"Where *are* we?"

His voice was fierce and edged with a foreign undercurrent of emotion.

Carmen's topaz eyes widened in surprise that the green-eyed boy should have to ask. "We are in the Underground, of course."

Greg glared at her. He didn't believe her. "Of course," he mimicked savagely, "and where on Earth is that?"

The girl in the white jumpsuit hesitated, uneasiness stirring within her. Something was wrong here. Why didn't he know all these things for himself? "It isn't *on* anything," she answered defensively. "It's Underground."

ESCAPE TO THE OVERWORLD

Nicole Luiken

Tree Frog Press
Edmonton

Tree Frog would like to thank the Film & Literary Arts Branch of Alberta Culture & Multiculturalism and the Alberta Foundation for the Literary Arts for their kind assistance. Special thanks to Arlene Birmingham, staffer, and Rudy Kendal, carpenter and proofreader.

Canadian Cataloguing in Publication Data

Luiken, Nicole.
Escape to the overworld

ISBN 0-88967-078-1

PS8573.U44E8 1988 jC813'.54 C88-091544-7
PZ7.L84Es 1988

Printed in Western Canada by D.W. Friesen & Sons Ltd.

5 4 3 2 1

Tree Frog Press Limited
McFrog Block, 10144 - 89 Street, Edmonton, Alberta, Canada T5H 1P7

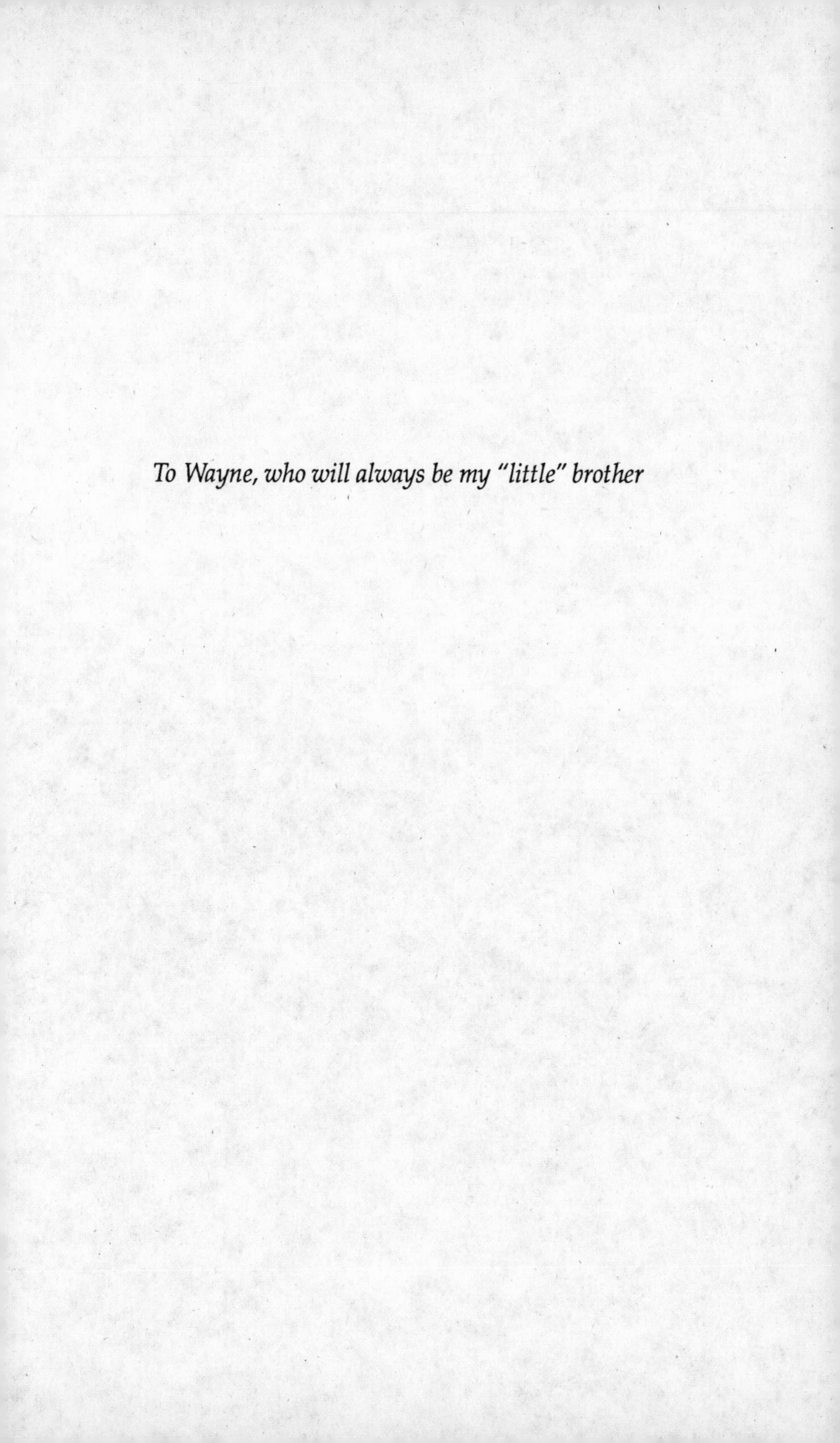

To Wayne, who will always be my "little" brother

Chronolog

Introhistory → → → → → → → → → 9

The Boy in Bed Three → → → → → → → 12

D comes before G → → → → → → → 21

The Choosing → → → → → → → → 33

The Empty Room → → → → → → → → 44

Removed → → → → → → → → → 58

Dream Drawing → → → → → → → → 66

Orange Sky? → → → → → → → → → 75

Escape → → → → → → → → → → 89

The Grand Overseer → → → → → → → 101

Underground Again → → → → → → → 110

Freedom → → → → → → → → → → 132

Glossary → → → → → → → → → → 139

About the Author → → → → → → → 142

Introhistory

Her eyelids were heavy, so very heavy.... But she must see! Somehow that thought was fixed above all others in her mind. Her lashes fluttered and light replaced the gray nothing of before. Then something else in the room stepped forward, throwing a shadow across her face. Metallic blue eyes flashed. "She is waking up," a voice said and a cold hand reached out to touch her forehead.

She remembered.

The girl lurched upright and off the table, bruising her hip in the process, but oblivious to the pain. She jerked free of the strong grasp of the one who held her and ran, blindly and without thought. Another of them loomed in front of her and she veered left, racing down a narrow corridor. Only when it was too late did she realize it was a dead end.

She hit the door full tilt, picked herself up and threw herself at its iron hardness again. Her struggles only increased as the footsteps came nearer and she beat at the door with her bare fists. The metal reverberated with her pounding. Vibrations went up and down her arm with each blow, but the girl did not let up.

Her pursuer stood behind her now, waiting silently for her to stop. In the end she did, sinking to the floor in a crumpled heap. She knelt there for a long time, shoulders heaving with sobs.

"There is no need for alarm," the low musical voice reassured her. "We will not harm you, Jenny."

Jenny stiffened at the sound of her name and, with an effort of will, swung her head to look at the speaker. Panic clogged her throat and it hurt to force the word out, "We?" She could not keep the horror out of her voice. There were more of Them. They were—inhuman.

The voice continued smoothly as though there had been no interruption. "It is our function to help, not hurt you. Unlike you humans, we neither practise nor approve of violence." The voice held a faint note of condescension.

But Jenny was past listening. "Who—what—are you?"

The creature did not seem surprised at her ignorance. "I am a Humanoid."

Humanoids! Jenny could not help but recoil. She had always thought—had hoped—that the old legends she had heard were just that: legends.

They were robots, creatures of wire and steel instead of flesh and blood. They had been invented by Earth's own scientists, over a century before, and had been hailed as the greatest scientific achievement of all time. They had been revolutionary, beyond compare, renowned from the beginning. But somewhere, something had gone wrong.

The Creators started to drop out of sight, one by one, taking with them all knowledge of their top secret invention. No bodies were ever found. Then, suddenly, within the space of a day, talk of the Humanoids dried up and the media stopped mentioning them. Those who remembered spoke of them only in the dark of night and in voices little higher than whispers. As generations passed, they became first like boogeymen, then the stuff of urban legends.

"What are you going to do with me?" Jenny's voice was flat with fear. There could be no going back. She realized that. She knew too much. She was a threat to the Humanoids' existence, just as the Creators must have been. Her stomach churned queasily. If only she hadn't decided to return early ... If only she had waited an extra five minutes ... the whole thing might never have happened. She would never have seen—what she had seen.

"You are part of the Underground now. Your needs will be met and you will remain here for the rest of your days."

The rest of her days. Never had words held such finality for Jenny, but she rallied quickly, getting to her feet, eyes roaming the room. She would escape from here. She *must* escape.

The door upon which she had been pounding slid open at the Humanoid's touch and she entered. For a moment she stood blinking in the sudden light, taking in her surroundings. The door closed noiselessly behind her.

Jenny whirled, suddenly panicked and flew at the door, prying with her nails at the crack where the opening once had been.

"It's no use," a voice behind her said. "Believe me, we've tried." Its owner, a young man of about her age strolled up. Then, as Jenny stared wordlessly, he extended a hand. "Welcome to the Underground. My name is David."

There were others as well: people of all ages who had been in the wrong place at the wrong time, who had seen too much for their own good. True to the Humanoids' word, their needs were all provided for. As far as comfort went, Jenny was better off in the Underground than she could have hoped to be in the tumult of the Cobalt Wars. But comfort only went so far.

The Underground was closely guarded: the only contact that Jenny, David and the others had with the outside world came when another poor soul arrived. Soon the trickle of Newcomers dried up. Life fell into a strange kind of monotony, each day exactly like the last, until they began to forget what the Overworld had been like. Their children were born to windowless walls and unblinking fluorescent light. They grew up knowing of nothing else. Their prison was their home.

CHAPTER ONE

The Boy in Bed Three

"Don't I even get a smile?"

The question startled Carmen so much that her hand on the linen stilled. The patient in Bed Three had been here for two days already and this was the first time he had spoken as much as a word. He had slept most of the time away. Now, up close, she marvelled at the clear green of his irises. What a strange colour for eyes! But then everything about this boy was different.

"Come on," he coaxed lazily, as if she were the patient and he the nurse. "Just one tiny, little smile?"

Hesitantly, she let the corners of her mouth turn up into the faintest of smiles. She did not know why. There was certainly nothing to smile about.

"See," he smiled himself, a wide grin that revealed two rows of oddly imperfect teeth, "I knew you could do it."

The C-chime sounded out from above, pleasantly low-pitched and thirty seconds in length. Carmen automatically finished folding her sheets and stacked them neatly on the shelf. Her shift was over, time for Meal B.

She was halfway to the door when his voice called out, "Hey, you with the sheets!"

She stopped, looking at him quizzically. He had half-raised himself up on one elbow. "What's your name?"

"Carmen."

She did not ask why he had asked; only two faint lines in her forehead betrayed her puzzlement. The question answered, she turned and continued to the door. She was one out of place in the line for the cleanser and would have to increase her stride slightly to make it to Meal B on time.

She did it, skimming down the halls with practised ease and passing her predecessor. Soon the muted talk of the Meal Room was upon her.

Carmen stepped up onto the scale in turn, watched it register fifty-two kilos, and grasped her plate firmly as the machine squeezed a medium-sized dollop of Food onto it. Her turn over, Carmen stepped neatly off the platform, picked up her glassful of Drink and took her place at the correct table.

The tables filled up rapidly with the exception of Donald's place beside her. This was not unusual. Carmen felt no surprise when he showed up with only seconds to spare, crammed most of the Food in his mouth with his Drink to follow, and finished before her. In the time that was left them, he enthusiastically filled her in on the details of his newest Project.

But today, as with yesterday, Carmen was not really listening. She was thinking about the patient in Bed Three. Even after Meal B was over and the C-chime sounded once more, her thoughts had not strayed. She wished that she could return to the Medical Ward instead of having to wait until the next day—a thought that was strange in itself. Projects had always been Projects, and their order had never made any difference one way or the other to her.

It was therefore just that much more of a disappointment to find the patient in Bed Three asleep when she arrived after Meal A the next morning. All throughout her shift, Carmen caught herself listening for his voice, and she even found the courage to ask Belle if he had awakened that day. He hadn't. Carmen went back to her job quickly, feeling a little flat.

Her eyes wandered over to his face again. Even before they had talked, he had held a peculiar fascination for her. His face was unnaturally brown (his medi-data said it was caused by a form of radiation overexposure) and possessed a kind of strength that puzzled Carmen almost as much as it intrigued her. His shoulders were wider than most. And his eyes were green.

Yes, Carmen decided, even had he not been a Newcomer she would have noticed him. He had a face her fingers itched to draw.

Carmen wrenched her eyes away from his face. It was not so easy to clear her thoughts of him or visualize what that hint of strength would look like drawn on paper. His name was Greg. She had checked his medi-data the first day he arrived. That would place him three down from her in lineup, in between Eleanor and Ilka. Donald was the only D and they had no F's or H's.

A little flutter of excitement ran through Carmen's veins. Her eyes wandered back to his face. There had never been a Newcomer here before. For as long as she could remember, there had always been thirty-nine Children; and once the Choosing had started that had decreased to twenty-nine. Greg would even out their numbers.

She was still watching him when his green eyes opened again. They saw her almost immediately and the glint of humour in them deepened. He looked straight at her, closed one eye, then opened it again extremely fast.

Carmen stared as he did it again. Was there something in his eye? She blinked her own as if to clear her vision. No, everything still looked the same. Feeling suddenly foolish, she bent back over her work. What did it matter if the Newcomer blinked only one eye?

"Hey, Carmen! Psst! Carmen!"

"Yes?" With the acquired calmness that had been taught her since birth, Carmen went to stand by his bed. "What do you want?" she asked. There were other nurses nearer. Why had he asked for her?

But he seemed in no hurry to answer her question, saying almost whimsically, "Carmen. The name suits you."

"Of course it does. It's my name." Carmen cocked her head to one side. What a strange thing to say!

"So? That doesn't mean a thing. Lots of people have names that don't suit them." He smiled once again over nothing that Carmen could reason out. "Take me, for example. You don't think I look like a Humphrey Matheson, do you?"

"Certainly not," Carmen replied, her confusion growing. "Your name's Greg."

"True," Greg admitted. "My name is Greg Matheson, but it might just as easily have been Humphrey Matheson. See what I mean?"

"See what?" Carmen asked. What was he talking about? And why had he called her in the first place? She wanted desperately to get back to her post.

"See that—oh, never mind." For the first time, the smile slipped from Greg's face and he dove under the covers.

He said no more, so Carmen took a step away, then paused, frowning. "Why did you call me?"

"Huh?" The covers came back down, mussing his dark hair. "Why did I call you?" Greg laughed without amusement. "Because you didn't come when I winked."

"Winked?" Carmen repeated, but apparently he was through answering questions; he had reburied his head under the pillow. She shrugged and went back to her readouts. The next time she looked, he appeared to be fast asleep. His arm was flung out above his head and his skin looked very brown against the sheet. For some absurd reason, her lips twitched upward into a smile again.

That day in Meal B, she interrupted Donald's talk about his Project, asking with an irrelevance that startled them both, "What does it mean, *to wink?"*

Donald paused mid-gulp, then shook his head, a shock of sandy hair falling over his eyes. "I don't know." His scientific curiosity aroused. "Why do you ask?"

"I'm not really sure," Carmen said, and in truth she wasn't. Sensing that Donald was about to press the subject, she hastily inserted a question about his Project.

"Ah, yes!" In matters like this, Donald was easily diverted. He happily and in great detail went back to telling her about his latest advances in Tri-Dynamics.

Carmen tuned him out. She thought that maybe, just maybe, if she were careful enough and finished all her work, she might get a chance to start on a drawing of Greg. One with his eyes open. Too bad she had nothing with which to colour them green.

The next morning, Greg's eyes were definitely open and his mouth was set in decidedly stubborn lines. He was sitting up, glaring angrily at the knot of Children surrounding his bed. "Carmen!" He caught sight of her over their heads and waved imperiously. She began to hurry despite herself.

Halfway there, she was intercepted by Belle. "What is it?" The words came out short and clipped. Carmen's eyes strained to see over Belle's shoulder. For a brief moment, she wished she were taller. That perturbed her as her height had never bothered her before.

"The patient has been healed," announced Belle. That's all, her tone seemed to imply, all in a day's work. "As a Newcomer, a tour has been arranged for him. However," Belle's brow furrowed slightly, "he refuses to go with Eleanor and has requested that you be his guide instead."

"May I?" A light burned deep inside Carmen's eyes.

Belle looked faintly surprised, as if the answer were obvious. "Of course. Why shouldn't you?"

But Carmen, inexplicably in a hurry, was already on her way to Bed Three. She nodded to Eleanor who looked relieved, nodded in return and went back to her duties. Greg's almost-grumpy expression vanished when he saw Carmen and he grinned at her. "Aren't you going to say hello?" he prompted.

Almost without her knowledge, Carmen's mouth curved into an answering smile. Its appearance was fleeting, however, and she said hello gravely.

"Hello yourself. As soon as I get my clothes and watch back, we can get out of here." He looked around hopefully as if he might find them sitting in plain sight.

Carmen had trouble understanding the first part of his greeting, but she chose to ignore it, ducking out into the Cloth Room. She reappeared minutes later with a soft, white jumpsuit of stretchy material. Except for the size, it was identical to her own and those of all the twenty-nine Children. "Here," she said, handing it to him.

But Greg did not want to take the jumpsuit. "Uh, sorry. There seems to have been some mistake. These aren't my clothes."

"No," Carmen smiled, "but you will wear this today."

The stubborn expression crept back onto Greg's face. "I prefer my old clothes." He kept his voice even.

Carmen tilted her head to one side, absorbing this. "Why?" She remembered the clothes he had come in. They had been coloured. Different. Intuitively, her mind leaped ahead. "Don't you want to dress like us?"

"Not particularly." His grim look stayed in place.

A "Why not?" was forming on Carmen's lips, but he cut it short, taking the jumpsuit out of her hands. "Forget it. I'll wear the stupid thing."

Carmen frowned over that one as he slipped into the change room. She had wanted to ask him why he had called the jumpsuit stupid when it wasn't at all. It was clean, useful and simple—all the things a jumpsuit should be. But something had cautioned her to keep quiet and she had.

The door to the change room suddenly crashed open. "What the hell is going on here anyhow?" Greg was examining his right temple in the mirror.

"What's the matter?" asked Carmen, rushing up.

"Where did I pick up this scar?" His green eyes sparked angrily, demanding an explanation.

"You were healed in Laser Surgery," explained Carmen, quoting from his medi-data, which now seemed lame.

After Greg had calmed down a bit, she coaxed him along the hall. They would retrace her usual route backwards and end up in the right room in time for Meal B.

Greg seemed to relax once they were alone in the hall and walked quietly beside her. He was on the wrong side of the white line, but Carmen took his Newcomer status into account and again said nothing.

The first room was Assembly. Carmen allowed Greg a minute to study its businesslike brown interior and chairs circling a hologrammer, before launching into an explanatory speech. "This is where we Assemble each morning for Project Updates, and every thirty days for Choosing." She was unused to the role of Program Director and Greg's silence unnerved her. She led him on through Meal A, Exercise and Washing before he spoke again. "Where is everybody?"

It was such an odd question that Carmen stopped to look at him. "The Children are at their Projects and the Chosen are still in Sleeping quarters. Where else would they be?"

Greg started to reply, then clamped his lips tight. "Never mind. How long before we reach the outside?"

"The outside?" Now Carmen was really perplexed. "The outside of what?"

"This building." It was Greg's turn to look at her sharply. "I've been promising myself a nice, deep breath of fresh air for the last two days."

Carmen disregarded his last statement. It didn't make sense. They were breathing ninety-six percent purified air right now. It didn't get any better. "This building," she stated baldly, "does not have an outside."

"What do you mean?" Greg shouted. He put his hands on her shoulders as if to shake the truth from her. "Where *are* we?" His voice was fierce and edged with a foreign undercurrent of emotion.

Her eyes widened in surprise that he should have to ask. "We are in the Underground, of course."

Greg glared at her. He didn't believe her. "Of course," he mimicked savagely, "and where on Earth is that?"

Carmen hesitated, uneasiness stirring within her. Something was wrong here. Why didn't he know all these things for himself? "It isn't *on* anything," she answered defensively. "It's Underground."

His green eyes were hard with anger now. "Where underground?"

"I don't know," Carmen admitted with something akin to shock. She really didn't know and, for once, there was no answer nearby to check. The Underground was her world and it had always been just that: the Underground. It wasn't on Earth or any other place. It was just—here.

Greg screwed his eyes tight shut for a moment, then opened them again. "Wait. Hold on just a second here. I seem to have misunderstood you somewhere along the line. Are you trying to tell me," he paused, framing his words very carefully, "that I am no longer in Tronno, that I'm in some underground hole in the earth?"

Carmen wondered at his last phrase *in the earth,* but stuck to what she felt was the main reason behind the question. "Yes, you are in the Underground," she repeated patiently. It did not matter that she had already said so before.

"But that's crazy!" Greg was about to go on, but when Carmen's face remained impassive, he clamped his mouth shut. His eyes locked onto hers as if willing her to retract her statement. When Carmen stared mildly back at him with her golden-brown eyes, he switched tactics. His voice remained compelling. "Look, we're not getting anywhere with this. Why don't you just tell me who found me in the first place and we'll sort it out from there?"

"Found you?" Carmen repeated blankly, then, at his impatient nod she resorted once again to bluntness. It was the only thing he seemed to understand. "Nobody found you."

Greg clenched his hand into a fist and absentmindedly massaged his knuckles. "*Somebody* must have found me," he emphasized. "I can't just have sprung up from the hospital bed like so much asparagus!"

"What's *asparagus*?"

He stopped fidgeting then, taking a seat at one of the tables and gesturing for her to do so as well. "Okay, Carmen, have it your way. If nobody found me, how did I come to be here? When did you first see me?"

This was easier, facts Carmen could deal with. "You were there when I came on four shifts ago." She saw the quick lift of his head and anticipated the question forming on his lips. "You were already in Bed Three. Fast asleep."

"Were you expecting me? Were you told the day before that another patient was on the way?" Greg leaned forward, his elbows on the table. His eyes never left her face. "Were you surprised?"

"No, no and yes," Carmen answered his questions in the order in which they'd been fired.

He pounced. "You were surprised to see me. Why? Don't hospitals get all sorts of different patients from the surrounding area and stuff?"

Carmen's head whirled trying to keep track. Surrounding area and stuff? What was that? "I was surprised because you are a Newcomer—"

"So?" he interrupted.

"So, you aren't one of us. We have never had—"

"We?" Greg's eyes all but glowed now. "Who's we?"

"We," Carmen repeated blankly. "We, the Children."

"Children of what?"

"Children of—" Carmen trailed off, confused. They weren't of anything. They just—were. She abruptly changed the subject, putting him on the defensive. "Why do you ask? Why don't you know?" Then, as a crowning effort, she fired back, "You should know better than me how you got here."

That stopped him. He almost seemed to shrink inside himself. The hand that came up to rub at his eyes was weary. "I should know, yes, but that's just the thing. I don't know. I have no idea how I got here. I don't know anything. The last thing I remember, I was joking with my friends after school." Greg frowned slightly. "Something about Mr. Levensworth, my Grade Thirteen chemohydrate teacher...." He shook his head. "Then nothing. Blank space. Until I woke up here."

Carmen was frowning now, too. "This *school,*" she hoped for the proper pronunciation, "where was it?"

"Tronno, Noram, Earth." When her face remained blank, he jerked a thumb towards the ceiling. "Up there."

Instantaneous awe descended upon Carmen. "The Overworld," she breathed. "Then it really does exist!"

CHAPTER TWO

D comes before G

"Of course it exists!" Greg snapped, half rising from his chair. "What made you think it didn't?"

Carmen avoided his gaze. Nobody had actually said it didn't exist. She had just presumed—as everyone else had presumed—that the Overworld's place was in the past, not the present. It would be a lesson to her: never draw conclusions without proof. "It's just that we hear so little about the Overworld," she said lamely.

"Well, believe me," Greg retorted, sitting down again. "Up there, in Tronno, you're less than a rumour—if that."

The word *rumour* was unfamiliar to Carmen, but she did not interrupt. It was important to listen right now, to absorb any information he might tell her.

His anger faded, to be replaced by a kind of despair. "Where am I?" It was a cry not to her, but to the very walls around them. He put his hands to his head as if it pained him to think. "What on earth has happened to me? And why can't I remember?"

Carmen had no answers and she offered none. She merely observed. The mention of *earth* again, for instance, was worth noting.

In the end, Greg did look up, his voice and gaze direct. "I want to talk to whoever's in charge around here. Where do I find them?"

Carmen blinked. *In charge?* What was *charge* and why did Greg want to see the person inside it?

Greg must have seen her confusion because he backtracked. "An adult. I want to talk to the adult in charge. Leader, boss, whatever." He was on his feet waiting impatiently.

Carmen was slower to rise. "I don't understand."

"Your parents! You do have parents, don't you?" He shot her a look that Carmen couldn't quite fathom.

"Parents?" she asked helplessly. Somehow she had all the wrong answers.

"Everyone has parents," Greg insisted, but his face went pale beneath its tan. Carmen hadn't known one could do that. "Your Mother and Father. Where are they?"

"Mother? Fath—oh!" The light dawned and Carmen forged ahead, reassured. "You mean my Factors. The ones who created me."

"Yes." He grasped at this straw eagerly. "Your Factors."

"But they aren't here." Carmen pronounced. Really, the Overworld must be an incredibly backward place if Greg didn't even know that.

"Then who is?" Greg remained persistent. The gaze of his eyes was oddly intent.

Carmen was about to answer when the C-chime sounded overhead. Automatically, she turned and headed for the first doorway.

"Hey, wait!" It was Greg at her elbow. He did not look pleased. "Where are you going?"

Carmen did not check her pace. They had talked far too long. "Hurry up. We're going to be late for Meal B."

"But what about my tour?" Greg kept walking beside her. He was on the wrong side of the line again. It was a good thing everyone was heading towards Meal B and not in the other direction.

"Somebody else will have to take you." Carmen felt a slight pang of disappointment. She had liked talking to him and explaining the rooms. This was the first time anybody had really asked her questions. Except for their varying Projects, what one of the Children knew, so did the others.

"What if I don't want anybody else?" Greg asked stubbornly, but Carmen had just come in view of the Meal Room and sped up. She was late, she knew it—though maybe not quite so late as Donald. As if in reproach the scale showed fifty-three kilos and her dollop was smaller. Her Drink, however, was bigger.

Behind her Greg stepped gingerly onto the scale. Carmen watched in amazement as the numbers kept flashing upward: eighty-one, eighty-two, eighty-three. It wavered there, then stopped. His Food consisted of more than a dollop, but Greg looked less than pleased when he finally picked it up and stepped off at the urging of the person behind.

"Do you really eat this?" Greg was looking dubiously from his glass to the white mound on his plate and back again.

Carmen gave him a strange look. "Of course we eat it!" What else would they do with it? Play with it?

Greg followed her to the table and sighed. "When they made me eat this goo before, I figured it must be hospital policy or something. All nutrition and no taste." He started to sit down beside her.

Carmen, who had been on the verge of asking what he usually ate, blurted out, "You can't sit there. That's Donald's chair!"

"Too bad."

Carmen watched helplessly as he settled himself in and started eating. She shot pleading looks towards Eleanor and Ilka, but although they had watched curiously before, their heads were now bent over their Food.

Carmen had trouble swallowing her Meal and was glad of the extra Drink in her glass. Donald, late as usual, was another minute or two in coming, his voice rushing as he said, "Hello, Carmen! You'll never guess what we did for Project today—" He stopped abruptly when he noticed someone was occupying his chair.

He looked towards Carmen for an explanation and she hastened to say, "This is the patient from Bed Three. He's a Newcomer. His name is Greg."

The temporary understanding that had flashed over Donald's face at the mention of a Newcomer faded when he heard the name. "Greg?" he repeated, his eyes going towards the vacant spot between Eleanor and Ilka.

"Yes?" Greg turned in his seat, his tone cool.

"You're sitting in my seat," said Donald, making a polite statement of fact.

"Really?" Greg's green eyes narrowed and he made a pretense of studying the chair. "I don't see your name on it."

"No," Donald admitted, two frown lines appearing between his sandy eyebrows. "My name is not on it."

"Good." Greg turned back to his Food.

But Donald, too, had a certain stubborn streak in him. "Are you going to move?"

"No." This time Greg didn't even bother to look up, his attention on his plate.

"You don't understand," said Donald, struggling to keep his patience. "You can't sit there. D comes before G. And besides—" in spite of himself, the anger crept in, "—I always sit by Carmen."

"Not any more you don't," Greg said coolly.

A slight red tinge came to Donald's cheeks. "Move out of my chair. Now."

"Are you going to make me?" Greg stood up. Carmen, who had always thought of Donald as fairly tall, estimated that Greg was over fifteen centimetres taller.

"If necessary, yes, I will make you," Donald frowned slightly. The problem was such a simple one; why did this Newcomer insist on having everything spelled out for him?

Greg smiled easily, lazily, and little prickles of alarm shot up Carmen's spine. She looked from one to the other. Something was going to happen, but what?

"Why don't you put down your tray, Donald?" Greg suggested softly.

Donald looked puzzled, but did as he was asked.

"Good." Greg's smile stayed in place. "Now then, you said you were going to make me move?"

"Yes," Donald agreed immediately. He was off guard and it showed. Who knew what this Newcomer might say next?

"Well then?" Greg's eyes mocked.

Hesitantly, Donald moved forward, laying a hand on Greg's shoulder. Then more confidently, he grabbed a good handful of white fabric. He pulled. Strangely enough, and it was this that Carmen always remembered later, the smile remained on Greg's face.

Seconds later, a swing from Greg's fist sent Donald reeling across the room. Ilka screamed, and a chorus of bewildered voices went up around them. The Children had never seen a fight before; not even squabbles were permitted.

One of Donald's hands went up to the cut on his lips and came away smeared with blood—just as red as the videosims in Anatomy had promised. His shock turned to anger. In an instant, Donald was back up on his feet and amazingly quick as he charged Greg.

From then on, there was a flurry of blows, both well-aimed and miscalculated, with most of the misses belonging to Donald.

Carmen should have been horrified, as everyone else was, but she wasn't. This lack within herself appalled her more than anything else. She tried to inject some scorn into her gaze. Violence, they had been taught, was evil and always bred more violence. But the condemnation would not come. Instead Carmen found herself strangely excited, exhilarated almost, because they were fighting over her. Over *her.* That was something that had never happened before.

The blood hadn't shocked her. Carmen hadn't screamed like Ilka had. In fact, she felt very little concern for Donald's safety at all: he wasn't the one she was cheering for. That too, alarmed her, for it made no sense. Things should always make sense.

She alone did not join in the collective sigh of relief that went up when the Humanoids came in to break up the fight.

Greg saw them first, his battle grin fading. He stood stock-still, one hand still clenching Donald's jumpsuit, the other pulled back ready to strike. Donald first twisted free, taking advantage of his opponent's stillness to land a blow of his own. Then, when this produced no reaction, Donald stopped, confused, and followed Greg's gaze over his shoulder. His arms fell limply back to his sides. He hung his head as one ashamed, as he of course had been taught from birth to be.

Greg was not. His expression spoke of many things, but shame was not one of them. He looked shocked, shaken, almost as if ... Carmen groped for understanding ... as if he'd never seen a Humanoid before.

That was, of course, impossible. Everyone knew of the Humanoids, of their great and continuous service to Humankind. Then why that flicker of some unpleasant emotion at the bottom of Greg's eyes?

Donald went with them docilely enough, but Greg came to life, recoiling violently when a Humanoid reached out take his arm. He punched at them in the same manner he had at Donald, but with little effect. Still, he kept swinging away, despite the pain he must have been inflicting on his bruised knuckles. He ignored the reassuring almost-human voice that repeated, "We will not hurt you," over and over.

Greg's eyes searched wildly for a way out, but there was none. Just before the Humanoids surrounded him, he appealed to the Children. "Help me! For heaven's sake, do something! Don't just stand there!" At the last, his eyes met Carmen's, asking—no—demanding her help.

Carmen took a half step forward and then retreated, her expression troubled. What was she doing? Her instinct was to go to his side, to help defend ... but against what? They had both wilfully participated in violence and Greg must be Warned. The fight must not be repeated. The Humanoids would know best how to deal with it. Sure enough, Greg was soon neutralized.

When the Humanoids escorted Donald and Greg out, the rest of the Children disbanded. It was with a distinct feeling of anticlimax that Carmen headed for her next Project. She would be late. Everyone would be late.

Somehow in all the excitement the C-chime had been ignored.

By Meal C, everything was back to normal, except that a subdued Donald was the one to sit in the seat beside her. And he was early, not late. Carmen hardly dared to look, but, sure enough, there between Eleanor and Ilka sat Greg.

He said nothing, but when he happened to glance up and see Carmen watching, his eyes burned with anger. Carmen went back to her Food with a snap. She did not look his way again. The fight was never mentioned.

Things stayed about the same in the days to follow, aside from a slight reawakening of interest in Donald for his Project. Yet things weren't completely the same. Carmen saw Greg at Meals and Assembly every day, saw him as she had never tried to see another. Her drawing enjoyed a rebirth. A particular face seemed to complete itself on the page, only to beg the start of another. The fascination of green eyes, radiation-browned skin and a scar held, even without the smile to bind it all together.

Greg stood alone, not listening, uncaring during Assembly. He condemned everything with his eyes and spent his time searching for doors and exits that had never existed.

Of all human traits, Carmen had been landed with curiosity and though she resisted valiantly for a number of days, it won out in the end. Against All Rules Of Course, she approached Greg during Rest Time.

She gave no greeting, just folded her legs up under her and sank to the mat beside him. Her request was simple. "Tell me about the Overworld."

"Why?" His green eyes narrowed suspiciously.

"Because I wish to know," Carmen said candidly. She did not mind his questions. She had gotten used to them, silly as they were.

"How do I know *they* didn't send you?" Greg's face remained harsh.

"They?" Carmen inclined her head questioningly.

"The Humanoids," Greg clarified impatiently. *"Them!"*

"They have not sent me," she assured him. Still, he did not seem to wish to speak. "Why do you not like the Humanoids?"

The reply was even quicker this time. "Why should I?"

Carmen frowned. "Because they have done so much for us. The Humanoids are our servants."

"Servants?" Greg snorted in disgust, forgetting to guard his tongue. "That's a laugh!" But he showed no signs of laughter, Carmen noted to herself.

"What do you mean?" she inquired, a mysterious warmth growing inside of her. This was why she had wanted to talk to him. He said the most unexpected things.

"I mean," said Greg, turning the full force of his eyes on her, "that they've got you so tied up, you no longer even know you're in prison! You wouldn't know how to escape if the chance were offered you."

"Prison? Escape?" Carmen picked up on the strange words immediately, a slight wrinkle marring her forehead. "Define them."

For a moment, Greg stared in disbelief, then he laughed. Carmen did not like this laugh. "How very thorough of them! They never got around to telling you. After all, how can you escape from your prison if you don't have the words for it? They don't take very many chances, do they, these Humanoids of yours?"

Carmen waited patiently until he got back around to her definition. He was the only person she knew who asked questions without answers. Fascinating.

"Prison is a place where you are held against your will. As for escape," Greg paused, squinting, "how about an action by which one flees something that is hazardous to their health?"

"There is nothing hazardous here to flee from. The Humanoids take good care of us," Carmen stated. "Your Overworld sounds far more dangerous."

"But at least up there we have our freedom!" Greg cried. "Down here you have nothing. You all wear the same clothes, speak the same way, your choices are made for you—" Greg paused mid-tirade and sighed. "You probably don't even know what I'm talking about, do you?"

"Not really. What is *freedom*?" Carmen's curiosity got the better of her. She did not believe Greg when he said they were prisoners. That would go against all she had ever been taught, but she found it very interesting. Her brain absorbed the knowledge like a sponge.

"Freedom is—oh hell!" Greg shut his eyes tightly and sighed. "How can I explain? Freedom means to be in charge of your own life, to be allowed to shape your own destiny." He paused thoughtfully. "It's a lot of things all at once, like you being the one who decides every morning what clothes you want to wear, and not having to obey a bunch of stupid bells—except during school hours, of course," he amended. "Am I making any sense to you?"

Carmen shook her head, ready with another question, but the aforementioned C-chime went. She swallowed her curiosity and started to rise.

Greg's hand on her arm stopped her.

"Yes?" she inquired politely. Her mind was already kilometres ahead of her in her next Project Room.

Greg must have sensed her withdrawal because his tone was oddly urgent. "Don't go, Carmen. Stay here and talk with me."

She looked confused. "But I have to go! The Bell—" she began unhappily.

"Blast the bell. And blast the Humanoids too," Greg grinned cheekily.

Carmen hesitated. The idea, after the initial shock had worn off, was oddly tempting. She remembered the day of the fight. Everyone had been late that day and nothing had happened. But to purposely not go at all! Carmen seesawed back and forth.

"Come on," Greg cajoled. "I'll tell you all about the Overworld."

That did it. Carmen sat right back down.

The last of the Children filed out the doors. Not one of them stopped to look back at the corner where Greg and

Carmen sat. Why should they? Everyone knew that when the C-chime rang, you went. Carmen shivered slightly. What was she doing here? She followed the departing Children with her eyes.

"So what did you want to know?" Greg intruded upon her worries.

"Everything!" Carmen turned to him eagerly. "Everything that you can remember."

"Remember?" Greg jerked back as if he'd been stung. "What makes you think I might not be able to remember something?"

Carmen's topaz eyes were limpid. "On the day of the tour, you told me there were parts of your life you couldn't remember," she reminded him. Had he forgotten that as well?

"Oh, right." Greg relaxed visibly. "I guess I did. So anyhow, what do you want to know first?"

That was easy. "What are the People's names?"

To her astonishment, Greg laughed. "Sorry," he apologized. "It's just that I have no idea what all their names are."

"Why not?"

He smiled again. "There are too many of them. I don't even know a fifth of the people in my own building."

"I know everyone in the Underground."

"Do you? Do you really?" Greg sounded amused.

"Of course. There's Adam, Belle, and me, then Donald, Eleanor and Ilka—" She started going down the alphabet.

"And what about the rest of them?" Greg insisted. "What about all your parents, or Factors, if you prefer? What about all your brothers and sisters? Do you know all the rest of the little equations the Factors made in different years?" He was, she sensed, teasing her now.

Carmen tilted her head to one side. "I suppose they would be a part of the Underground as well, wouldn't they?"

"I imagine so," Greg said dryly. "I find it hard to believe that thirty kids could be born in one year and none in the next."

"Thirty-nine," Carmen corrected automatically. He had neglected to count the Chosen.

"Where I live—" Greg pointed upwards, "—each family lives separately in an apartment of their own."

Carmen had no idea what a *family* was, but she felt this was not the time to interrupt and sat contentedly listening. Her reactions were mirrored perfectly on her face and Greg used them as a guide, picking his words with care, trying to make her understand.

"A family is a group of people that has two Factors and a varying number of kids." He glanced at her to make sure she was following. "Or I should say, children, but not your kind. What I mean is— Forget it. In my family, there are only four of us. Mom and Dad, of course, then me and Lucy. Lucy's only twelve."

"Twelve what?" This time Carmen did ask the question out loud.

Greg stared. "Twelve years old."

"And what is a *year?*" Carmen leaned forward. There was so much for her to learn.

"Three hundred and sixty-five days. They haven't told you much, have *they*?" Again that contemptuous referral to the Humanoids. "What *have* they taught you?"

Carmen thought for a moment. The only thing that came to mind was her Project which dealt with the refinement of lasers. There were the rates of absorption and physical effects of radiation, but that was kind of simple. She settled for rattling off Einstein's equation for microscopic reversibility and her own theory that light absorption and emission occur at equal rates. "Of course," she added, "that's only true in the steady-state situation."

"Of course," Greg agreed in a strangled voice. He cleared his throat. "I guess you do know a bit after all! You learned all that in Project?"

The awed expression on his face made her lips twitch, but Carmen controlled the impulse to smile. "I learned it ten shifts ago," she admitted. But at the moment, Projects did not really interest her. "Tell me more about the Overworld," she prompted.

"Well, Dad works as a Carbolics Co-ordinator and makes good money—" He caught her eye and sighed. "*Money?* Money is what you are paid for doing your job and what you use to buy the things that you need to live."

This seemed a little silly to Carmen. Why not get Food in exchange for the work? She started to say so, but Greg just smiled. Carmen smiled as well; she couldn't help it. That was when the doors opened again to the Assembly.

They both became very still in their corner. Carmen found herself holding her breath without reason.

The Humanoids said very little. They called her name and, as if pulled by invisible strings, she came. When Greg said something, from way back in his corner, she started to turn, but the Humanoids' grip on her arm prevented her.

"We will not hurt you. We will not hurt you," the voices said. Carmen relaxed. They were words that had been used to sing her to sleep, so how could she resist? Like a trusting lamb, she let them lead her out the door.

She did not notice when the needle was produced or flinch as the pink liquid in it was expertly injected.

"Now then, Carmen," the voices soothed in harmony, almost like music, "why did you Disobey the Bell?"

CHAPTER THREE

The Choosing

Catching a glimpse of taffy-coloured hair ahead of him, Greg opened his mouth to yell "Carmen," then stopped. The past three times he'd tried to catch her attention, she'd turned in the other direction. At first he'd thought she just hadn't heard him but, hey, three times was three times.

Grimly, he started to push his way through the crowd of Children. They didn't push back, just stepped around him. That bugged him. They weren't normal. Just look at what they called themselves—The Children. Greg grimaced in disgust. They were no younger than he was and Greg had not considered himself a child for years.

The whole Underground bugged him.

At first when Carmen had told him where they were, he hadn't believed she'd meant it—not literally at least—but after a week of looking for exits or just the simple existence of a window, he was ready to accept it. They were Underground. Buried by tons of earth and probably a few buildings nailed down over top.

The thought gave him an awful smothering sensation, and the Children crowding him didn't help either. Why were they all going in the opposite direction as him anyway? He wasn't on the wrong side of the line again, was he? Greg took a look to the left and groaned. He was. No wonder Carmen had gotten ahead of him so fast while he hadn't gained much ground at all.

Oh well, too late now. He turned and walked with the Children. Might as well go with the flow, he told himself wryly. He didn't have a lot of choice.

In fact, as he saw it, the Humanoids had made darn sure he didn't have any choice. Their first appearance, shining metal creatures that they were, had shocked him more than he was willing to admit. There was nothing like them in the Overworld, as robots there were tiny, went on wheels, and were only capable of limited functions. Artificial intelligence, beyond that required to serve drinks, was not one of them. But Greg felt uneasy even as he thought this. There had been some kind of association his mind had dredged up at first, some part that was not just startled, but afraid.

He didn't buy their "We-will-not-hurt-you" stuff. If they weren't going to hurt him, why keep repeating it like that? The Humanoids might have the rest of the Children brainwashed, but not him. Not Greg Matheson. That was one of the reasons he found it so hard to believe that he had ever come down here of his own free will. There, of course, lay the crux of the whole problem: why was he down here? And why couldn't he remember? The thought brought on a wave of homesickness.

When he had first awakened, it had been easy enough to identify his surroundings. Soothing pink walls, white-uniformed people—it *had* to be a hospital. He'd presumed his loss of memory would be temporary at most, but here it was going on three weeks and he still didn't remember anything past talking to some friends after a normal day of school. If he had his memory back, Greg was almost positive he'd be able to escape this—this overgrown burial plot!

What could have happened to him during that blasted blank space in his memory? The possibilities were practically unlimited. Good atoms, he didn't even know how long he'd been out of it. Hours, days, months. *Years*. His reflection told him it couldn't have been much longer than that. He didn't seem to have changed much physically. That was a plus.

The Humanoids knew what had happened to him, of course; that was another reason for hating them. For a while after the fight with Donald, Greg had thought that all the Children—Carmen included—were in on the deception, but her innocent question on what the Overworld was like had convinced him differently. And she was quite free with her knowledge of the Underground. Greg had been on the verge of asking her—casually, of course—if she knew of any way out when the Humanoids interrupted.

They'd taken Carmen away, but only favoured him with a cold stare and a Warning. He'd waited impatiently for the next Meal to continue his conversation with Carmen, but Greg had been unable to catch her alone since. Three times was three times. She must be avoiding him. Greg set his jaw. The next time he saw her he was going to get to the bottom of this—and fast.

But Carmen, it seemed, had other plans. She could move surprisingly quickly. Only by dint of running did he manage to catch up to her. Everyone stopped where they were and stared at him. What were they all looking at? Hadn't they ever seen anybody run before?

Carmen's first words when he pulled up beside her answered that one. Her eyes were wide as she demanded, "How did you do that?" She, too, had stopped to stare.

To his surprise, Greg felt his face growing warm. "Uh, it's called running. We do it all the time up in the Overworld."

Something flashed across Carmen's face that was strangely like fear. Strangely, because in all his weeks here, even when he'd threatened to bash a few faces in, nobody had seemed in the least afraid. Without thinking, Greg asked, "Why are you afraid?"

A puzzled look came to Carmen's eyes. "*Afraid?* What is *afraid?*"

Greg's features relaxed into a smile. This he could handle. "To have fear. That's to, um, show anxiety because you're being threatened."

More frowns. "Nobody is threatening me," she pointed out, "therefore, I cannot be afraid."

"I guess." Greg had no argument against logic like that.

The conversation over, Carmen turned to go. "Hey, wait!" Greg cried, catching her arm just above the elbow.

"Ouch!" She flinched visibly and snatched his fingers away, rubbing at the flesh.

"Sorry. Let me see." Gently, Greg removed her fingers and looked at the white skin on her arm. Before coming to the Underground, Greg hadn't known such pale skin was possible. Then he saw the marks. Greg sucked in a breath and his face got angrier and angrier. He swore under his breath and pulled Carmen to the side, out of traffic.

For once, Carmen knew better than to ask the meaning of the words, inquiring only, "What is it?"

But Greg was not listening; he was furious. "They did this to you, didn't they? Some peaceful robot?" he glared at her. "And don't say 'Did what?'! I'm talking about the needle marks."

Greg glowered as Carmen looked in apparent surprise at the line of red punctures marching up her arm. "Well," he demanded, "did the Humanoids do that to you or not? Those marks certainly weren't there last time we talked!"

Carmen made no response other than tipping her head to one side in typical fashion, so he fired off a few more questions, his anger now just as much directed at her as at the Humanoids. "Is that why you've been avoiding me? Because of this?"

Carmen's eyebrows went up. "Have I been avoiding you?" She considered for a moment, then answered her own question. "Yes, I must have been." This thought seemed to trouble her a little; two small lines etched themselves across her forehead.

Greg folded his arms and waited, frowning.

Seconds passed, then Carmen stepped back out into the corridor and started walking away—fast. She paused, and Greg's heart lifted, she turned slowly looking a bit uncertain, as if about to ask something of critical importance. "Greg, will you show me how to run?"

His face broke into a smile and he jogged right up to her. "Sure. There's nothing to it." Sports was something Greg had always excelled at. It would take no more than a few minutes to teach her the basics of a good stride.

She was off.

"Remember, stay on your toes!" he shouted after her.

She didn't say thanks. Nobody in the Underground did, but she smiled and that was enough.

Slowly, reluctantly, Greg turned in the other direction. He had some running of his own to do, if he wasn't going to be late either. Last time he had gotten the distinct feeling he was excused because of his Newcomer status, but if he should slip up one time too many.... It wasn't that Project was so terrible; after the first few weeks of cramming and catching up, it was actually kind of interesting. He just didn't like being told what to do. He never had, and to be told by a stupid robot was even more galling.

Greg waited for Carmen at supper time, or Meal C as everyone else called it, but although she replied politely to all his questions, she was careful to keep some distance between them. And she smiled at Donald.

Over the next few days Greg grew increasingly frustrated. He wasn't used to this kind of treatment and certainly hadn't expected it—not from Carmen. Flat-out refusal he could handle, but indifference? Never. He knew she was curious. After all, she'd been the one to approach him that day they'd Disobeyed the Bell.

She had Disobeyed the Bell. That said a lot. In the Underground all the Children had been trained since birth to eat, breathe and *move* when that chime went.

No, it had to be something else. The Humanoids. Those needle marks on her arm!... Just thinking about it made Greg's temperature rise. Carmen wouldn't even admit it was the Humanoids that had given her the needles. Remember, Greg told himself savagely, the Humanoids were peaceful, nonviolent creatures, weren't they? He wished he had something hard to punch. Or at least space to run as hard as he could for as long as he could. He felt so helpless. How could you help a person to see, if they wouldn't even acknowledge that they were blind?

It was that thought which plagued Greg the most as he stared moodily across the room at her. She was sitting beside Donald. Sometimes, like now, he wondered why he didn't just give up, go chase after another girl. But he knew even as the idea formed in his head that he wouldn't.

They were in the Assembly Room, sitting in perfect rows, legs crossed, backs straight, eyes glued to the front. The thought impinged on Greg's consciousness that something was a little different about today's meeting. He made a deliberate effort to listen. This was more than Progress Reports, though there were those, too. There was something different present in the room today, as if everyone were waiting for the routine to be over with. Greg's gaze on the Children sharpened. He hadn't seen them so alert-looking since the day of his and Donald's fight.

"Today is the day of the Choosing," a Humanoid announced. That was different too. Generally they were present, but silent.

Apparently everyone else knew what was going on because they all rose in unison, separated into two groups—one boys, one girls—and arranged themselves into a semicircle.

Greg thought about leaning over to the boy sitting beside him and asking him what was going on, but the boy's unusual expression stopped him. He looked strung out—absolutely tense, as if he had been waiting for something a long, long time and the suspense was killing him. He looked *alive,* as opposed to the Children's usual vacant state.

Intrigued, Greg leaned forward slightly so he could hear. What was going on?

A Humanoid opened things up by pointing to the first boy at the top of the circuit. Silence reigned. The boy shook his head.

The mechanical finger moved on to the next boy. Another negative. Then the next, this time a yes. The boy stood up, his voice wavered, he said a name. The girl to whom the name belonged rose. The couple stepped to the side. The finger moved on.

Greg began to smile. He'd been wondering how to get ahold of Carmen alone. Here was his chance. He began to coil his legs beneath him for an early rise. Greg glanced around surreptitiously. Donald was on the other side of him. Good. He'd get his chance first.

It was the turn of the tensed-up boy beside him. He nodded violently and sprang up like a released spring. "Eleanor," he blurted. A tall, thin girl from across the room arose, and joined him. Greg vaguely remembered her as sitting beside him at Meals.

Finally the finger turned to Greg. He nodded confidently and stood up. "Carmen," his voice rang out. He was so busy looking triumphantly at Donald that he quite failed to notice the shock that flashed across Carmen's face before she got to her feet and glided forward.

They met halfway in the middle. Greg dared to take her hand as they went on to the side. No words were said, but Carmen's golden-brown eyes were glowing. Who needed to smile when your eyes could do that?

Greg turned his eyes back to the proceedings. Donald, he was happy to notice, looked so pale as to be almost sick. He shook his head when his turn came. After the finger went all the way around with no more nods, the Children broke up, down only six in number. This disconcerted Greg slightly, why only six? Had he missed something somewhere? Oh well, too late now. Greg shrugged the thought off, and looked with some eagerness towards the approaching Humanoids. Now what?

But the Humanoids passed by without a word. Greg was beginning to feel distinctly uneasy, as if he'd walked into Act Three of a play without a script to go by. This feeling was heightened when he looked around to discover the other two couples were gone.

Greg decided to make a stab at jauntiness. "Well, what are we waiting for?" When that failed to elicit any response other than a blank look from Carmen, he resorted to bluntness, dropping all pretense. "Carmen, what did I just do?"

Carmen shot him an incredulous look from underneath her lashes, but she answered obediently enough. "You just Chose me."

Greg tugged at his brown hair. "I know that! But Chose you for what?"

This time it was Carmen's turn to stare at him openly. "Chose me!" she repeated with far more emphasis than Greg had seen her display before. "You Chose me. Forever!"

The significance of what had happened dawned on Greg. He took an involuntary step forward and peered hard into her face. "Forever? Are you telling me we just got—" he swallowed hard, "—just got married?!" The thought was mad, incredible. All he had done was nod and say her name!

"Chosen," Carmen repeated warily. "We are Chosen. Once two more couples are Chosen, we will become Factors and advance one level."

"I don't understand." Greg blocked out her words, turning abruptly away from the clear gaze of her eyes. This couldn't be happening to him. Disbelief warred with the almost certain knowledge that Carmen would have no reason to lie. "How could this have happened?" he turned on Carmen, suddenly angry. "How could you have let this happen? You knew what being Chosen meant." His green eyes bored into hers. "Why didn't you stop me?"

"I did not wish to stop you." Carmen's reply was simple, utterly truthful. Again the glow was in her eyes.

Greg's anger left him as suddenly as it had come. "Oh," he said. He could think of nothing else to say. The first thought which struck him was that he wouldn't have to worry about Donald again—ever. For such a small thing, it gave him a rather large amount of satisfaction. He'd gotten up there, calmly Chosen Donald's girl, and Carmen hadn't said a thing to stop it. No wonder Donald had looked sick!

Greg grinned, but only for a moment. There were other questions that needed to be asked.

"Two more couples, you say? How long might that take?"

Carmen shrugged. "It depends. The next Choosing isn't for thirty days, and even then, two more might not Choose."

Something almost like disappointment hit Greg. He camouflaged it under another question. "Why five couples?"

Carmen was exasperated. "It would be inefficient to advance a group with any less."

"Of course," Greg mocked, "and one must always be efficient. I'm surprised the Humanoids let you Children Choose at all. I would have expected them just to run a list through the computer and let it come up with the appropriate names in alphabetical order!"

"Choosing is hardly a logical process," Carmen explained seriously, as if rehearsing an argument she had heard many times. "It will work properly only if the individuals decide for themselves, no matter how haphazard this process may seem. Please keep in mind we are dealing with human beings, not robots."

Greg listened, wide-eyed, then burst out laughing. "In other words, they did try it once, but it turned out to be such a total flop they had to give it up!"

The bewilderment on Carmen's face grew and she looked at him as though trying to solve a particularly difficult puzzle. She saw nothing to laugh about. "The only restriction put on Choosing has to do with Factors. If too many Factors are already shared between a couple, they cannot Choose each other."

Greg's brow knotted. "I'm afraid I don't know what you mean."

She elaborated. "My Factors are C, D, J and R. I cannot Choose anyone with those letters."

"Like cousins, you mean?" Greg was quick to ask, but when she didn't appear to understand, he raised another question. "Who could you have Chosen from?" Something had just occurred to him. Donald's name began with D.

Carmen rattled them off alphabetically. "Adam, Ken, Ned, Peter and, of course, you. There were more, but they've already Chosen."

An irresistible urge to laugh hit Greg. All that worrying over Donald who was some kind of relative and not even in the running! The joke was on him.

His mirth seemed to upset Carmen, however. He'd never seen one of the Children even close to angry before. She said stiffly, "The Choosing is not a laughing matter."

"Sorry, I wasn't laughing at you. What's this about advancing?"

Carmen steadied. "You asked me once where everybody else was. They are on different levels. Once we become Factors, we will be promoted to a higher level."

Faint stirrings of excitement started inside Greg. He kept his voice deliberately calm. "Do you mean we will be going up there?" He pointed to the ceiling.

"Not yet," she replied matter-of-factly. "We will remain at this level until our Factor Group is complete." She looked at him curiously, "Weren't you told?"

"They didn't tell me anything—at all!" His green eyes burned hate. He was going to get out of here and, if being Chosen meant getting that much closer to the surface, then he'd do that too.

Fingers touched his arm. It was Carmen, concern etched upon her face. She said nothing, but the question was there in her eyes: "What are you thinking?"

Greg shook himself, forcing a smile. "This is crazy, you know. Here we are engag—Chosen and we haven't so much as kissed!"

Her head tilted slightly, her eyes quizzical. "Define *kissed*."

Greg's face broke into a wide smile. He couldn't have planned it better himself. "This," he said gently, "is a kiss." He gently tipped up her chin and sealed her lips with his.

She did not step back as Greg had half-expected, but instead stayed perfectly still until he drew the kiss to an end. "Oh," she said, on a long note. Her eyes were wide and vulnerable, the pupils larger than normal.

Deeming it wise to change the subject, Greg picked up an earlier thread. "And this upper level, is it the top one or is there a higher one yet?"

"There are two higher, I think." Carmen frowned with the effort of trying to remember. "They are not much spoken of."

Greg crossed his fingers. This could be it. "How do you get there?"

But this met with a blank wall. "I don't know." So did most of his other questions on both the Factors and other levels. The level below Children was Babies and Carmen remembered little about it. Not knowing what years were, Carmen could not tell him exactly how long they had been here other than "a long time."

Greg knew the feeling. With only Bells, Meals and Sleeptimes to separate things, days tended to blur together in the Underground. He had made a point of scratching a line into the smooth plastic by his bedpost every Sleeptime. The Underground, of course, had no night. The lights burned constantly.

Overhead the C-chime rang. To his surprise, Carmen did not get up immediately. "The Chosen ones are allotted more time," she explained. "We do not have to go yet."

"Well, we might as well go anyhow. Unless," Greg's eyes filled with mischief, "you wish to practise up on some more kissing?"

To his absolute astonishment, Carmen rose and said gravely, "Yes."

"Yes what?" Greg floundered, momentarily off balance. He had only been teasing.

But Carmen was dead serious. Why else would she have said it? "Yes," she repeated patiently. "Kiss me."

CHAPTER FOUR

The Empty Room

Carmen was trembling slightly when the kiss ended and this alarmed her. Was she coming down with one of the Sicknesses? No, there was more to it than that. This feeling inside her had started long ago. It was only when Greg had called out her name as his Chosen that it had manifested itself fully. Her insides had turned to stone when Greg first stood up at the Assembly. As he had not Asked her beforehand, she had thought he had Chosen someone else. When he spoke out her name, the little thing that had died within her burst back into life.

At the time, she had given little thought to his not Asking—it hadn't mattered. It still didn't. Carmen's lips stretched into a smile.

"You're beautiful." Greg's soft-spoken words broke the spell. He hadn't meant to say them—they had just slipped out.

Carmen frowned reprovingly, saying as she had always been taught, "Beauty is the most foolish of all human values."

Greg looked startled, then annoyed. "Says who? Your precious Humanoids? I don't see where they have much right to criticize. All they are is a walking bucket of bolts!"

Carmen should have been shocked, but she wasn't. Hadn't she known when she'd made the remark in the first place that Greg would resent it? She had wanted to hear how he would defend himself. Her curiosity was getting the better of her again—another all-too-human trait.

But now was not the time to pursue it. Their extra time was almost all used up. Although she would never admit it to Greg, Carmen had taken another look at those puncture marks on her arm, and thought long and hard about their possible origin.

"To what Project do you go now?" she met Greg's gaze levelly.

"Tri-dynamics. Why?" The suspicion was back on his face.

Carmen was sorry to see it and she kept her tone absolutely natural. "I will go with you." Then at his surprise, "Yes, it is allowable for the Chosen. Tomorrow you may come with me instead."

He offered no argument, simply taking her hand and showing the way. There was enough room for both of them on the right side of the white tape, but Greg seemed to take perverse pleasure in straddling it, now that no one was around to see. Carmen said nothing, but her eyes were shining again.

She sat beside him at Meal C. Eleanor had gone to sit beside her Chosen, so the seat was there for the taking. Donald, she noticed, was in surprisingly bad humour, not even mentioning his Project. But it was Greg who claimed her real attention and once her tasteless mound of Food had been devoured, she occupied herself with watching him. Up close, she noticed there were several little things she had missed in her drawings—like how red the tips of his ears were turning.

"What is it?' he demanded at length, his ears fully red now. "Have I suddenly grown two heads?"

"Of course not." Carmen drew back a little. The questions he asked!

Greg sighed loudly and went back to his Food. It was only afterwards when the Bell had rung and the people were clearing away that he spoke again. "This allotted time," he began, putting his head quite close to hers, "exactly how much of it is there?"

"An hour a day."

"Only?" Disappointment showed plainly on Greg's face and Carmen warmed inside. He wanted it to be longer.

She tried to look on the bright side. "We still have half an hour."

"Wonderful," Greg grumbled. "And I suppose it'll have to be the Assembly Room again."

"Yes." Carmen hesitated slightly. Should she tell him? No, not yet. She needed more time first. They walked there hand in hand and once they sat down, Carmen turned to him impulsively. "Tell me about the Overworld."

Greg looked uneasy, undoubtedly remembering the last time she had said those words and the Humanoids had come to break them up. But then they had Disobeyed the Bell.

Her curiosity had not been nearly satisfied last time. Carmen could not imagine why she had not asked him again the next time she had seen him—some kind of Warning perhaps, but that seemed very vague and unsatisfactory now. She turned her eyes to Greg. "Tell me"

And so he did. Carmen listened with rapt attention as he described his life with its skyscrapers and the strange thing called Government. He told of its people and of his friends. Of a thing called Fashion and more of Money, which made the world go round. This was news to Carmen. She thought it had something to do with gravity, but when she told Greg this, he just laughed.

Greg went on to tell her a smattering of history, all about the Cobalt Wars and, most fascinating of all, the Overworld. There he had seen the most wonderful things imaginable—and so strange that Carmen almost suspected him of making them up. There was Sky which was blue and roofed the Overworld and a Sun to light it by day and a Moon by night. There were scientifics behind both these phenomena, but Carmen could not really take it all in.

She also gathered, by what Greg told her, that the Overworld was a much bigger place than the Underground she knew. The half hour was well past by the time they left. Tomorrow's hour would have to be docked some.

The Humanoids were waiting for her when she got back to Sleeping Quarters. "Hello, Carmen."

Not a word was spoken about her being late. None was needed. But all that she had ever been taught about the

Humanoids and the Overworld was reviewed. Fact by irrefutable fact, the wall that Greg had broken through was built up again. Without the Humanoids' ever mentioning his name, Greg was branded a liar.

"We only want to help you, Carmen," the musical voices told her.

Do you? Carmen asked silently. She didn't feel as if she were being helped, but, of course, the Humanoids would never lie. Usually their words and their familiar voices effectively dispelled all doubt. But this time, although convinced, Carmen felt, well, almost resentful.

They had been listening in on her and Greg. The Ears in the Underground were so much a part of life that Carmen rarely remembered them; but today—probably because of Greg's words and, by extension, his thoughts—she thought of them and wondered at their purpose. Didn't the Humanoids trust her? Carmen made a hitherto unknown leap in the dark, using Greg's words to do it. If the Humanoids were in the right—which, of course, they unquestioningly were—*what were they afraid of?*

Of course, such thinking was silly as well as nonproductive, so Carmen turned over and slid smoothly into the world of Sleep.

Her greeting to Greg the next morning was grave. Neither her eyes nor her mouth smiled.

Greg took one look at her and assumed a glum look himself. "I see they paid you a visit, too."

Carmen did not pretend ignorance. "Yes." She was not surprised.

It was all they said. Project had started.

Theoretically their forty-five minutes extra could be taken at any time, but it wasn't until after Meal C that the subject came up.

"The Assembly Room again?" Greg's tone held more than a little trace of bitterness. His visit by the Humanoids must have alerted him to the existence of the Ears. Carmen had seen him studying all the walls around very carefully.

Unless pointed out, they were hard to find. Ears must be another thing the Overworld lacked.

"Not if you don't want to go there." Carmen's voice was not quite steady. But he was her Chosen. He must be shown.

"Where then?" Greg's eyes met hers, curiosity in their depths.

"Wait and see." Carmen could not speak of it now. Secrets, once told could never be retracted. She led the way, going straight up to the corner and pressing down on a certain point until, silently, the two walls drew apart revealing a tunnel. Carmen kept herself pressed up tight against the wall. This was the only tricky part, getting past the Eye; after that, it was smooth sailing.

She had done it the first time through sheer luck. Carmen had always been smaller than the rest of the Children and she had been able to walk unnoticed down the middle while the Eye skimmed over her head. Donald being taller had not been so lucky.

Greg asked no questions, seeming to appreciate the secrecy of the route.

And it was secret. Not even the Humanoids, Carmen was sure, knew it was there. If they did, she would never have been allowed to go there. Not alone anyway. No Child was ever left alone. To do so was unhealthy. It was a proven Underground fact that Children did not learn when left to themselves and often cried when they were. But not Carmen. Above everything else, she valued privacy. She did not quite know why she wanted to share her secret with Greg, except perhaps because it was *her* secret. Carmen frowned to herself; she wasn't making any sense.

They rounded the last corner and there it was—just a simple room, not even one fifth the size of a normal one, done up in none of the Humanoid's mood-making colours. Just white walls and white floors.

Greg whistled under his breath, his admiring eyes taking in the room before coming to rest on Carmen.

"Nobody else knows about it, do they?" he said, stating a fact more than asking a question.

Carmen answered him happily enough. "Nobody." Donald had known once, but he did no longer.

"Good." The smile almost split his face and his laugh sounded good echoing off the walls. "No, it's more than good—it's fantastic!" Greg started walking around its perimeter, running a hand over the smoothness of its walls. "I wonder what it was built for?"

Carmen started to reply that she had no idea, but Greg had already moved onto the table in the centre of the room and the paper and pencil on it. "These yours?" he asked, picking them up casually. "There seem to be quite a few of them."

"No!" The word was torn from Carmen's throat. She sprang forward, pleading, demanding. "Do not look at them!" She grabbed at his arm.

He held them easily out of reach, his brows drawn together by a frown. That suspicion again. "Why shouldn't I look? What are you hiding?"

Carmen stopped at once, her arms dropping limply once more to her side. How could she have been so stupid as to bring him here?

Greg was looking at them now, his face showing his shock as he looked at the first, crudest drawing she had done. It was greatly wrinkled. She had drawn it when she was supposed to be doing Project and, upon its discovery, the Humanoids had disposed of it as they did with all the Imperfect. "It has no practical application," they had told her. Both holography and photography could reproduce such images far more accurately and faster. Carmen had had nothing to say in defense, her eyes watering and her head hanging, but that didn't stop her, later on, from rescuing it from the Disposal Tray and bringing it here.

Greg was flipping through the pictures faster now while Carmen studied the floor. She could not bear to see his face when he found the latest batch of drawings—the ones of him. Shame was heavy upon her. Carmen could feel water welling in her eyes. The drawings had always brought her joy, so this exposure was doubly shameful.

The paper rustlings stopped and Carmen supposed that he must be done looking at them by now. The silence stretched out.

"Carmen," Greg said, his voice sounding oddly husky, "I don't know what to say."

That broke the spell. Carmen's head came up. "Then I will say it for you. I am evil. I was Warned before and must be Punished now. And I don't care if it *is* wrong! I would do the same thing all over again!" Her topaz eyes sparked defiance.

"Good for you!" Greg's words held genuine approval. To Carmen, who had been expecting shock and horror, they were more worrisome than an accusation would have been. The Children had been taught to regard drawings with extreme loathing.

"What do you mean?" She looked at him sharply.

"I mean," said Greg, pausing deliberately, "that these drawings are the single most wonderful thing I've seen since coming to the Underground. Disobeying the Bell was a step in the right direction and the secret room here is another one, but these pictures—" Greg held them up, "—they really say it all. The Humanoids can't win!"

Carmen frowned, unsure of what he was trying to say, not that it mattered. Her last bit of courage fizzled. She had Disobeyed a Warning not once, but over twenty times. Carmen gave one last longing look towards her pile of drawings, before turning away. "We might as well go now," she said in a tired voice. "If I say I'll never come back here again, will you not tell the Humanoids?" Carmen could not bear the thought of her drawings once more being Disposed Of.

"The Humanoids? Carmen, wait!" It was Greg at her elbow, exasperation tingeing his voice. He pulled her around and forced her to look straight into his eyes. "You've misunderstood me." He smiled disarmingly. "Listen to me; I like your drawings. They're good, really good. They have—" he searched for the right word, "—expression!"

"They are a waste of time and have no purpose." Carmen's voice was flat, rehearsed. "It is wrong to waste time. It is wrong to draw." She would not be fooled now. "It is evil."

"It is not!" This time Greg's face showed signs of real anger. "And you will not say so again! Listen to me," his voice gentled. "You're an artist. There's nothing wrong in that. It's a talent. Up on Earth we put such drawings in galleries for everyone to come and see. The artists get paid money for it."

Money. Carmen remembered that. It was the payment you received for doing your work so that you might get your Food. "It's wrong," she repeated stubbornly. The words had been hammered into her head for as long as she remembered. "The Humanoids say so."

Greg's next words threw Carmen for a loop. They were low and dangerous. "And why are the Humanoids always right and I always wrong? They're only machines!"

Carmen had never thought of it that way. "I, I don't know," she sobbed.

Greg saw his advantage and pressed it. "Look, Carmen, I know that you've only known me a month or two and the Humanoids have been around all your life, but just for once will you listen to my side of the story? That's all I'm asking, I swear it. Now will you?"

Ever so slowly, Carmen nodded. He was her Chosen and she could not refuse.

"One day I'm up in the Overworld, talking to my friends and not doing anything I haven't already done twenty times before, and then whammo! I wake up in the hospital. Not only have I lost part of my memory, but I find out I'm in some forgotten place called the Underground. I didn't ask to come here, but some tin-can excuses for robots are holding me prisoner against my will! Yes, prisoner," he repeated more strongly, having seen Carmen blanch when he said that word.

"And you're just as much a prisoner as I am. Think about it. You've never been given any kind of power over your own life. Your Food is set in front of you. Your bedtimes are arranged." He waved at the wall. "Heck, you don't even have light switches! You've been cut off, deliberately cut off, from the rest of the world. And any attempt on your part to break free of the mould they've laid out for you is Punished. They may claim to be *nonviolent*," he spat the word out contemptuously, "but they're not above using threats and needles to get their own way. Face it, Carmen. They've been brainwashing you since day one."

But Carmen shrank from such a confrontation. She did not wish to choose between Greg and the Humanoids. Greg was her Chosen and the Humanoids her World. And yet, one of them was Right and the other was Wrong.

"Well?" prompted Greg.

"There is so much," she began haltingly, "that I do not understand." Her eyes were troubled. "There are the Humanoids," she acknowledged, "and there is this." Carmen put a hand up to her mouth where Greg had kissed her.

To her surprise Greg's face went mottled crimson.

This time her curiosity got the best of her common sense. "How do you do that?"

"Do what?"

"Change colour." Carmen looked on fascinated as the red deepened. She had once read about a Lizard that did that, but never a person.

"It's a talent of mine." Greg's voice sounded all weird and choked.

Carmen let that one pass, her thoughts switching back to the decision before her. She looked up at Greg almost in desperation. She wanted very much for him to be in the Right. "How do I know who to believe? How do I choose?"

"It's easy." His voice sounded warmer and he put his arms around her, allowing her head to fall back against his shoulder. "Just listen to your heart instead of your head."

"My heart?" Carmen looked up at him from under a strand of falling hair. "The heart is a muscle that pumps my blood and carries oxygen to all the parts of my body. How can it tell me?"

"Shhh" Greg said. "Just listen."

She did. There were two heartbeats now, going in and out of rhythm. It seemed oddly beautiful and very special—not in the least foolish.

It was Greg who first said, reluctantly, "We'd better be going soon."

"You will say nothing to the Humanoids about my drawings?" she asked anxiously. She did not want to lose that privilege.

"Oh, I think that could be arranged," Greg said airily, "for a price, of course."

The puzzled look fell over Carmen's face again. Didn't prices have to do with Overworld money?

"Don't worry," Greg said. "It's a very small price. Only one kiss."

"Oh," Carmen smiled in relief. "Just one?" She stepped closer to him, putting her arms around his neck.

"One or two," Greg grinned wickedly, "or three or four."

In the days that followed, nothing was said of their discussion, but Carmen knew she could not afford to wait too long. She must make up her mind soon. Greg or the Humanoids. The Humanoids or Greg.

One particular comment of Greg's bothered her, the one that mocked the Humanoids' stated policy of nonviolence. Her arm was still sore from the needles she had been given. The balance swung momentarily in Greg's favour, then back again. She had been trained to study a problem from all angles before drawing conclusions. And this was no problem to be taken lightly. She must be sure.

Methodically, Carmen began to work out a method to test her hypothesis. Greg must know nothing of it. These things had to be done properly or not at all.

Still, on the day before she was to begin the experiment, Carmen drew him to one side after Assembly and silently led the way to the Empty Room. She had something to say and, for reasons she did not attempt to understand, she did not want the Ears to hear.

"What is it?" Greg looked at her curiously. This was not her usual behaviour at all.

Carmen met his gaze levelly. "In the past," she stated formally, "I have asked you to define many words for me. Today I have a definition with no word to express it."

"Yes?" Greg cocked an eyebrow, waiting.

"It is a feeling. A kind of joy, only not like joy. Bigger, better." Carmen's forehead knotted as she struggled to explain. "It grows by the day, by the hour and spills out even onto the empty ones. It is strongest when I am with you, but it does not weaken while you are away. It is the most precious thing I have.... Do you know what I am talking about?"

"Yes." Greg hesitated. "I think so. It's called love."

"Love," Carmen repeated. Her face cleared and she smiled, both with her eyes and her mouth. "I have love for you."

For a moment Greg looked as if he might say something in reply, but instead he put his arms around her. Carmen didn't mind in the least.

It was only later, when he had left, that the doubts returned. She decided, then and there, to put her plan into action. Instead of sneaking below the Eye as she had always done, she walked directly in front of it, slowly, so that there would be no mistaking who she was. Then she waited for the Humanoids to come.

They were there within minutes, grasping her firmly by the elbows and walking her in the direction of the Assembly Room. They said nothing and despite her conviction that this was the only way to find out, Carmen began to feel anxious. Of course it was impossible for the Humanoids to hurt her. That would go against everything the Children had been taught. But, still the uncertainty persisted. What if Greg was right? Carmen's throat went dry. One thing and one thing only was for sure: by the time this night was over, she would know who had lied.

The Assembly Room was empty and when they got there Carmen was steered to the middle of the floor and parked between two Humanoids. Their metallic blue eyes began flashing, sending strange patterns onto a white part of the brown wall.

Carmen waited impatiently. What now?

Then, slowly and noiselessly, the entire floor began to sink. Carmen stiffened, unprepared. On either side of her, the Humanoids remained perfectly still. Soon an interruption on the smooth surface of the wall began to appear. When the full length of a doorway was uncovered, the Humanoids started for it, walking in 4/4 time and pulling her along.

Gleaming metal surrounded them on six hexagonal sides. This must be the Control Room for the whole Underground, Carmen thought to herself. It was certainly big enough. Dozens of Humanoids walked blindly past them, set on their own duties. The flashing computer consoles somewhat resembled those in the Children's Computer Project Room, but on nowhere near such a grand scale. Carmen looked around in awe. Flashing lights cast blue and violet pools which were reflected many times over by the gleaming metal surfaces.

"Hello, Carmen." The voice in front of her, neither friendly nor unfriendly, brought her back to herself with a start. She had deliberately broken a rule and her Punishment was being decided. Carmen's head came up and she met the Humanoid's eyes directly.

"Why did you go into a restricted passageway?" The question was deceptively simple, but Carmen trembled. She could not tell the truth about her experiment and bring up Greg's name. He was already on Warning for both the fight with Donald and the Bell—a third report could be disastrous. She kept quiet.

"You were seen coming out of the passageway, but not going in. It is logical to conclude that since you knew the passageway was restricted, you avoided the Eye on purpose." The voice was condemning. Carmen's face flushed and she hung her head. Things were getting out of hand. What had she done?

"You will not go into the passageway again." The words were final, hammered into Carmen's brain with absolute conviction. "You will forget that it exists."

It took all her strength not to nod her head, and an extra effort to speak. She must find out. She must know for sure. "What will happen if I do go back?"

Her question was met with silence, save for the slight whirring noise as the Humanoids considered. "You would not like it," it said at last.

Carmen's blood froze. That had sounded a lot like a threat to her. "What would you do?" she repeated. "Would you harm me?"

Again she received no answer, but suddenly she realized none was needed. Greg had been right! The Humanoids were quite capable of harming her if they felt it in their interests. Carmen felt tears well up in her eyes and their presence made her unreasonably angry. "So it's true then. The Humanoids are nothing but a pack of liars!"

The whirring stopped. One Humanoid spoke to another as if she were no longer there. "The damage is more serious than we first thought. She has begun to think dangerously. Such thinking dates back to when she Disobeyed the Bell. It was suggested then that the Newcomer Greg, by whom she was Chosen, contaminated her. This has now been confirmed."

Carmen's breath caught in her throat. What had she done? If she had gotten Greg into trouble as well, she would never forgive herself.

Its next words chilled her even more. "Suggestion: certain memory circuits, those dealing with the time period since the Newcomer first appeared, must be erased."

There was another slight pause, then the response almost stopped her heart."Confirmed." A distinct metallic click punctured the silence. Carmen looked down to see that a hypodermic needle had sprung out of a compartment in the Humanoid's hand. Glinting in the eerie light of the hexagonal room, it began to move towards her face while other metallic hands, at her wrists and arms, kept her from twisting free.

Panicked, Carmen started to scream. "Greg—"

CHAPTER FIVE

Removed

"Where's Carmen?" Greg's voice was hoarse, his eyes wild as he laid a hand on Donald's shoulder. "What have you done to her?"

Donald looked up politely from his Project, then, when he saw who was speaking, bent his head back down. "I don't know what you're talking about."

"Like hell you don't!" Greg yanked him off his chair, slammed him against the wall and glared at him eye to eye. "Now tell me where Carmen is or I'll break your jaw!"

Donald studied Greg warily. He had nothing to tell him, but it did not seem prudent to say so right now. It was not a matter of courage, but of common sense. He had just gotten rid of the bruises caused by their last fight and had little desire to acquire some more. The fight hadn't been one-sided by any means but, judging from the expression on Greg's face, this fight would be to the death and the variables were not in Donald's favour.

"The last time I saw Carmen was at Assembly last night. She was standing with you. You two left before I did." Donald pronounced each word clearly. He wished to take no chances of being misunderstood.

Greg swallowed convulsively, releasing his hold on Donald's collar. His anger drained away only to be replaced by an awful sense of loss. "That was the last I saw of her, too," he whispered.

After leaving Assembly, they had gone to the Empty Room. It hurt now to think of that. Sweet, truthful Carmen who had come right out and said what he hadn't the courage to. "I have love for you." This morning, for the first time since coming to the Underground, Greg had woken up happy—so happy that he had almost been unable to believe his good fortune. It had come as a very nasty shock not to be able to find her in the Meal Room.

"Perhaps," Donald suggested, "Carmen is waiting for you at Project."

Greg glared at him, eyebrows white with anger. "Don't you think I would have checked there already?" After choking down as much Food as he could manage, he had scoured the Underground, starting and ending with the Empty Room in case Carmen had come in while he was gone. "She's not there." The panic showed in the edges of his voice again. "She's gone!"

A small chill went up Donald's spine. He offered no reassurances, crossing over to speak with the dark-haired girl who was programming on the next keyterm. "Ilka, do you know where Carmen is?"

Ilka did not seem surprised by the question. "Carmen was Removed last night." Her tone was quiet, as one might speak of the dead.

Donald recoiled, his pale skin turning paler. He had hoped it wouldn't come to this.

Greg jumped in. "*Removed?* To where, and by whom?" His green eyes held Ilka's intently. He was on his feet, ready to run if need be.

Ilka swallowed uncomfortably. "By the Humanoids, of course, and it is not for us to know where."

"The Humanoids." Sick certainty swept over Greg. This was all his fault. The Humanoids were his enemies—not Carmen's. His face hardened and he kept his voice even with effort. "What does it mean, *to be Removed?*"

Donald seemed reluctant to answer, so Ilka took it up. She faced him curiously. "Don't you know?"

"If I did, would I be asking?" Greg practically growled.

"Probably not," Ilka admitted, frowning. "That would be a waste of time."

Greg tried again. "What does it mean?"

Donald spoke this time, tiny spots of colour beginning to reappear in his cheeks. "It's a Punishment," he explained. "If you Disobey too many Warnings, you are Removed."

"For how long?" Greg shot the question out.

Donald and Ilka exchanged glances.

"How long?" Greg demanded. He was almost gnashing his teeth now. If he didn't get some answers soon, he felt he would go crazy. "You must know. Others must have Disobeyed before!"

"Yes, they have," Ilka replied with what seemed like to Greg infuriating calmness. "Most are Returned." She glanced sideways at Donald.

Greg's face went unnaturally white. Only most, not all. "How long before most are Returned?" he asked. His hands were clenched into fists and he was sweating, an almost-unheard-of occurrence in the Underground where the temperature never changed.

Ilka considered. "Usually within ten hours," she said at last.

"And how long has Carmen been gone now?" Greg felt ready to explode. A lot could happen to a person in ten hours. The alarm bells were getting louder inside his head with every second. Why didn't she just answer?

Ilka consulted the digitime on the screen of her keyterm. "Thirteen hours, seventeen minutes."

Too late! Greg agonized for a few precious seconds, then turned to Donald, his mind made up. "How exactly does one set about getting himself Removed?"

"Disobey a Warning." Donald looked first confused, then genuinely horrified as he realized Greg's purpose. "But you can't do that!" he blurted.

Greg's facial muscles didn't move an iota. "Watch me." He may not have known exactly what he was doing at the time, but Carmen *was* his Chosen and nobody, but nobody, was going to take her away from him.

He left Donald and Ilka standing by their machines. Greg didn't think he'd have much trouble getting himself Removed. He'd already shown a remarkable aptitude for breaking the rules. Not showing up for Project had probably already given him a head start.

With Carmen gone he didn't have a whole lot to lose. Most of the Children wouldn't even miss him until tomorrow and Greg seriously doubted that anyone would be at all surprised. He was a Newcomer. They had raised no fuss over Carmen; why should they over him?

"Stop!"

Greg turned and saw with some impatience that Donald was following him, walking as fast as he could. He did stop, but only because Donald might have some useful information concerning Carmen.

"What are you going to do?" puffed Donald when he had caught up with Greg.

"I'm going to Unremove Carmen," he declared. "Oh, don't worry." Greg held up a hand. "I'll be sure and ask the Humanoids politely first."

"They won't let you," Donald said on a calmer note, walking along beside him. "You know that, don't you?"

"That's okay," Greg smiled icily. "I have a plan for that, too. The first Humanoid that gets in my way, I'll dismantle piece by piece." Greg cracked his knuckles. He would enjoy doing that. "Care to come along?" he invited Donald mockingly. "It'll be fun."

Donald didn't smile. "Don't do it. You'll only make things worse."

Greg's temper got the better of him. "Worse? How much worse can things get?" Raw misery gnawed at his gut. "They've got Carmen. Doesn't that mean anything to you? Don't you care?"

"Of course I do," Donald shot back with more feeling than Greg had seen from him since their fight, "which is exactly why I'm trying to stop you from getting yourself Removed!" His voice softened a little. "That would be absolutely the last thing Carmen would want to see happen." He paused to let his point sink home. "Carmen will be Returned."

"When?" Greg ground the word out from between clenched teeth. She had been Removed for thirteen hours now; his throat closed tightly. Removed. He hated the word more with every growing minute. "When will she be Returned?"

Donald shrugged helplessly. "I don't know. As Ilka said, Removees are usually back within ten hours. Those are for minor wrongs. Carmen must have done something more serious."

"That's another thing!" Greg interrupted angrily. "I've broken more of their stupid rules in my month here than Carmen has in her lifetime. If anyone should have been Removed, it was me," he ended morosely. He had a horrible feeling this whole thing was his fault.

Donald said nothing to disagree, just repeating his opinion that Carmen would be Returned and that it would save time later on if Greg stayed put. "When she comes back, she'll need all the help she can get. As you know, having your memory erased is not pleasant."

Greg froze. The only person he had told he had amnesia was Carmen and it hurt to think she might have passed the news along to Donald. "Who told you?" he asked roughly.

Donald gave a blink of surprise. "No one told me. I noticed your scar."

Greg was momentarily at a loss. "So *that's* why I can't remember!" Then his thoughts shuttled back to Carmen. "Are you saying they'll erase her memory, too?"

"Yes." Donald faced him squarely. "And when she comes back, you must not tell her anything that she has forgotten, for as soon as she remembers she will be Removed again."

"They've got the perfect solution, haven't they?" Greg asked bitterly. "It's like turning back the clock at will. Just erase a person's memory and anything that shouldn't have happened, won't have."

"It's better that way."

"Better than what?" Greg lashed out. "How would you know what it feels like to be missing a chunk of your life?"

"I know," Donald said steadily, "because I was Removed once." He pushed back the sandy hair on his forehead to reveal a small scar.

There was a moment of silence before Greg smiled. "Well, well, well. Whadda y'know? I should have known you had guts when you actually started hitting back in the Meal Room."

"Guts?" The expression of puzzlement on Donald's face was almost comical. On any other day, Greg would have laughed. But not today.

"Bravery, courage," he defined without thinking.

"Stupidity," Donald added to the list. "I was almost Removed again for it. Violence is never the answer."

Greg shot him an impatient glare. "And you don't consider wiping out someone's memory violence? Grow up. The Humanoids have been stringing you along for years."

Donald looked as though he was going to protest, but the C-chime sounded. The Children swarmed in an orderly fashion towards Meal B and Greg allowed himself to be carried along with them. The piece-by-piece dismantling of a Humanoid would have to wait for another day. Donald had been right on that point. It would be stupidity. Still, Greg gave the Humanoids five days to Return Carmen. Any longer and he was going in after her.

Waiting for anything had always been difficult for Greg and the added suspense made it nearly impossible in this case. Without Carmen around, he ended up talking to Donald more often than anyone else and got a bit clearer picture of what the Underground was like to live in. He didn't dare talk of the Overworld with the Ears listening in, but Greg did do his best to widen a few cracks in the Humanoid's perfect facade.

It was just after Meal A on the fourth day when Greg caught sight of a familiar taffy-coloured head, walking past the door in the midst of several silver Humanoids. Greg got up from the table so fast his Drink spilled. "Carmen?" His voice came close to breaking over her name.

Her head swivelled so that he caught a glimpse of pale cheeks and topaz eyes. It was her. The initial wave of relief that swept over Greg died as he saw the Humanoids rush her past.

"Carmen!" Greg broke into a run, dodging the Humanoids and Children alike with ease. He hadn't played International Tag for the Tronno B.J.'s for nothing.

The Humanoids became alarmed, their blinkers going first red, then orange. "Do not disturb the patient," they told him.

Greg ignored them and called out to Carmen again. This time she turned and Greg could see a puffy, red welt on her forehead. Her eyes locked with his for a full second. Carmen's stricken expression was so different from the last time he had seen her that he was already skidding to a halt when Donald tackled him from behind. They both toppled over.

When Greg came up from underneath, Carmen and the Humanoids were already rounding the corner. He made a move as if to go after her, but this time it was the Humanoids who blocked his way.

"Do not disturb the patient," one said.

"But that's Carmen!" Greg protested, eyes swinging from the corner behind which she had disappeared to stare uncomprehendingly at the Humanoid that was speaking. "She's my Chosen."

"Not anymore," he was informed in a mild voice. "Carmen no longer remembers you." The Humanoid clicked off after her.

"Well, that's the end of that," Donald said regretfully. "They must have erased her memory of more than just a few days."

"That's the end of nothing!" Greg said violently, green eyes stormy. Then, when Donald looked questioningly at him, he tried to explain. "I can't just switch my feelings for Carmen on and off like a videosim!"

Donald looked puzzled, but spoke quietly. "Nobody's asking you to switch off. The fact remains, Carmen doesn't remember you. For her, the past thirty days haven't happened. But it's not the end of the world. You're no farther back than you were thirty days ago."

Greg moved away morosely. "It was a long thirty days."

CHAPTER SIX

Dream Drawing

She was mad. She must be mad! The proof of her madness was right there, staring Carmen in the face.

It was bad enough to have a Dream—the same Dream five nights in a row—and everyone knew what Dreams meant. But this, this was the end. She had not even the cloak of Sleep to hide behind. Her eyes were wide open, now dilated in disbelief at what she had done, at the drawing she held in her hand.

Carmen had been horrified when she woke up and was told by the Humanoids that she had been Removed while she slept. Had it not been impossible for the Humanoids to lie, she would not have believed them. She had trouble accepting it even now. She, Carmen, Removed? It did not make sense. Nothing did.

One day she had retired to bed after a perfectly normal day, uninteresting in the extreme and the next, to waken to this. Time had supposedly passed in the interim, but she could not remember it. The Humanoids thought it better that way.

The knowledge gained in Project while she was gone had been Overprinted and, in the three days following her operation, she had reviewed the material several times to make sure nothing had been missed. Only in one thing could she pinpoint a difference between life before and life now. The Dreams.

These were not the pleasant, vague Dreams she had enjoyed in the past and managed to forget almost immediately upon waking. This Dream refused to be banished. It remained, lurking in the corners of her mind, ready to catch her off guard in some moment of weakness. Like now.

The images in them were vibrant, larger-than-life and they filled her with a nameless emotion that made her sit up in bed afterward, staring and shaking violently. Once she had even screamed, so that a Humanoid had come to sit beside her and asked if she was in pain. But all Carmen could do was dully shake her head. A Dream that was not forgotten meant mental instability and she was not ready to admit to that yet.

The Dream was the same from night to night. She was locked inside herself, unable to move or speak, only feel. Her body was controlled and directed by a will that was not her own. The feeling of helplessness was overwhelming. She could see a boy on the outside, trying desperately to bridge the gap between them. His lips moved, calling her name but she could neither hear him nor reply. Cruel hands reached out and pulled him back out of her vision and, then, the same hands came towards her, blotting out the Dream entirely.

It was the Boy who stayed in her thoughts the longest afterwards, the wildness of his expression always wrenching at her in some strange way. Carmen was sure she had never seen him before in her life and, yet, he was the only part of the Dream that she did not regret upon waking. He was oddly real to her and Carmen almost felt that she should know his name. He looked different than the Children, taller, stronger and his eyes were green. His whole face showed an animation she had never seen in any of the Children. She had managed to capture a hint, just a hint, of this depth in the Drawing of him she now held in her hands.

It was unmistakably a drawing of the Boy. Carmen had finished her Project assignment for the day and, feeling unusually restless, idly picked up a pencil. She had extra paper as well and, again without thinking, she began sketching lines on the paper. The lines had evolved into a head, as was usual, because there wasn't much else worth drawing in the Underground.

When Carmen was pretty much finished, she held it back a ways, squinting at it critically. Not bad, the verdict came out, though she had done better. That scar for one thing; she'd messed up on it rather badly. Her eraser had been poised over the picture, intent on correcting it, when she first saw exactly who it was she had drawn. The Boy. Complete unto the minutest detail.

Carmen began to shake. There could be no other explanation for it. She must be mad.

She was on the verge of crumpling the Drawing when she heard the unmistakable sound of Humanoid footsteps approaching and shoved it in her pocket instead. It would never do for the Humanoids to find her wasting time on Drawings.

She was to Return to the Children's level next morning and the thought both exhilarated and frightened her. Carmen didn't like being one of the Removed, but she was also unsure of how she would be treated when she got back. The other Children would know more about her past than she did. What if she had done something horrible? By the time the next morning rolled around she had a definite case of the jitters. A repeat of her Dream hadn't helped either.

She was escorted back upstairs on a curious rising floor that ended in the Assembly Room. Two Humanoids marched in front of her and two in the back. The procession made her feel self-conscious, but it had been timed to coincide with the serving of Meal A so there were only a few seconds she was actually visible.

"Carmen!" Her name, followed by a crash, made her turn her head. The scene in the Meal Room looked reassuringly the same, with the Children all in alphabetical order eating their Food and Drink. With one exception. One boy was standing up, staring after her in such a way as to make Carmen feel extremely uncomfortable. She had a feeling she should know him, but, for the life of her, Carmen could not remember his name. The thought that he must be one of the things she had forgotten upset her. Then she took a few more steps and was past the doorway.

"Carmen!" Her name was called again, this time with such urgency that she had to turn and see who it was.

The all-enveloping light of the Underground outlined a face that was oddly familiar and emphasized the strange green of his eyes.

Carmen let out a strangled gasp, fortunately covered by the steady tramp of her Humanoid escorts. Her hand went to her mouth in what could have been either shock or dismay. It was the same boy who had been standing up inside the room. This time Carmen knew at once why he had looked so very familiar.

It was the Boy from her Dream.

The Humanoids ahead of her kept walking while the one behind dropped even further back. She heard a loud thud and gave one last backward glance before turning and blindly following the Humanoids ahead. Her thoughts were in turmoil. The boy who called her name had been lying on the floor this time and Donald of all people had been holding him down. What in Einstein's name had she forgotten anyhow?

The Humanoids did not stop until she arrived at next Project. She was given stern instructions not to try to find out the reason behind her Removal. "Anything that you have forgotten should stay that way."

Carmen found herself nodding rather absently. Her thoughts were still back on the boy. Who was he? Not one of the Children surely? She had known them all since birth and her memory erasure only went back about forty days as near as she could calculate from the amount of Project material that had been reviewed.

The rest of the Children from Project filed in, but the New Boy was not among them. Carmen did not quite dare ask anyone who he was. Her Removal was a bit of a touchy subject and she wished to avoid even mentioning it. Besides, her reasons for asking were rather personal and not for sharing. With a desperation that alarmed her, she wanted to see him again.

Carmen could not understand herself. She did not know this boy—but she Dreamed of him. She wished for another look at his face. But she had drawn it from memory without trouble. Perhaps it was better to be mad, after all....

Her chance to meet him came quite naturally at lunch time. He sat beside her. At first, her eyes flew to where Donald stood in the Food lineup, but when he sat down and started talking to Ilka, she relaxed slightly.

"Hello." The green eyes smiled at her. "My name is Greg, and yours, I know, is Carmen."

Carmen almost asked how he knew, but stopped in time. "Yes." She inclined her head slightly. "That is my name." She was exceedingly curious about this Greg and kept glancing at him out of the corner of her eyes while she ate. More often than not he was staring right back at her.

He didn't talk as much as Donald, but when he did, it seldom had anything to do with Project.

"What is this stuff anyway?" Greg poked dubiously at the white mound of his plate.

Carmen frowned slightly. "It's Food," she said, stating the obvious.

"In whose definition?" Greg mumbled before taking another bite and washing it down with Drink.

"The Humanoids, of course." Carmen was so busy watching Greg that she quite forgot to eat her own Food.

"Easy for them to say," Greg complained. "They aren't the ones who have to eat the stuff." He wiggled one eyebrow at her so that, quite in spite of herself, Carmen found herself smiling widely. She could not have said exactly what was so funny about wiggling an eyebrow, but it was, and, when he did it again, she laughed.

As laughter was virtually unheard of in the Underground, she immediately became the focus of everyone within hearing distance. Even before her giggles stopped, Carmen ducked her head slightly, taking a hurried mouthful of Food. When she looked up again, Greg was watching her with an expression that could only have been of satisfaction.

"I'll have to remember that," he said lightly.

Carmen studied him with golden eyes as if trying to fathom a particularly hard puzzle. "Remember what?" She had a hard time understanding much of what Greg was talking about half the time. She always seemed to be questioning him.

Greg didn't seem to mind. "Remember that you smile when I wiggle my eyebrows."

"But why—" Carmen started to ask, then cut herself off. Her curiosity was getting out of hand again.

Still, Greg seemed to know what she was going to ask. "Because I *like* to see you smile." His voice dropped again, became husky. "And your laugh is beautiful to hear."

Carmen dropped her eyes in confusion. Nobody who she could remember had ever said that to her before and she was at loss as to what to reply. Everything the New Boy said seemed to be double-edged, to have two meanings. Carmen sighed. She had the feeling she was missing something here. It was probably the fault of that dratted Removal of hers.

The C-chime went, bringing Carmen to with a start. Her plate of Food was by no means finished. The only thing she could do now was down the rest of her Drink in a single gulp. Greg waited for her and motioned for her to go ahead of him in the line. Such behaviour was puzzling, but Carmen made no protest. It was with reluctance that she left him to go to Project.

Laser Healing was very intense that day, requiring all the powers of concentration the Children had learned. Still, Carmen found her mind wandering off topic and to Greg more than once. It was with quick, swift steps that she made her way to Meal C afterwards. She wanted to see Greg and she had to fight hard against the urge to speed up, bend her legs more at the knee. To run.

Carmen stopped short then, feeling the blood drain from her face. She almost panicked. What had she said? *To run?* What kind of a word was that? But she knew what kind of word it was. That was the trouble. Run was not a word they had been taught, nor an action done in the Underground. Yet Carmen knew of both.

Greg was already in the Meal Room. He waved to her, lips stretched into a welcoming smile that Carmen returned without thinking. It was really very strange, she thought as she sat down beside him, how different he appeared among the other Children. In fact, had she been asked to describe him in one word, that would have been it: different.

By now she had come to the conclusion that he had not been of the original Children and he must have arrived somewhere during the time she had forgotten. There was another assumption that could be reached at the same time—that he must have had something to do with her Removal—but Carmen pushed the thought out of her mind for the time being. She didn't want to know.

She started off by asking him which Projects he was in and what they had done that day.

"I'm in Tri-Dynamics and Engineering,' he said impatiently. "Today we did an experiment involving controlled curvatures in flight and the effect of the Cobalt Wars on nuclear power. There. Now can we talk about something important?" he snapped.

Carmen was a little taken aback. What could possibly be more important than Projects? But she nodded and conversation resumed.

"Okay." Greg smiled again. "First things first. Are you doing anything in particular after Meal C?" Carmen shook her head and Greg's face became more serious. "Good. Would you come with me then, please? I have something to show you."

Carmen's curiosity was immediately aroused, but she sensed by the look on Greg's face that this was exactly what he wished her to feel, so she smoothed her face into a pleasant mask. "I will come."

She ate all her Food this time, she noted, and although Greg talked and wiggled his eyebrows a lot, he was quite silent about the "something" he wanted to show her. Carmen played along and asked no questions, even stopping to talk with Ilka and Donald a bit before leaving the Meal Room with Greg.

As Greg led the way in the opposite direction of the Exercise and Activities Room, she watched him first with interest and then with growing apprehension. She slowed her pace. There was nothing here but Projects and ... something she didn't like. When Greg reached the corner that opened up into the Empty Room, she balked entirely. "No! I won't go in there. I won't!"

Greg looked at her with surprise and a little bit of speculation. "So you do remember," he murmured, "at least that much. Of course, you knew of the room long before you showed me."

Carmen became suddenly very still. She felt as if she were standing on the very edge of a cliff. "I showed you?" she repeated.

"Yes." Greg looked at her levelly. "You showed me, just a few days after we were Chosen."

"Chosen?" Carmen felt her limbs go weak. "You and I were Chosen?" Her eyes mirrored her bewilderment. "But I don't even remember you!"

"I know." Greg's eyes became suddenly fierce. "The Humanoids did that to you. One of these days they're going to pay for it," he vowed.

Something in his tone told Carmen that someday he would do just that, and she shivered, backing away. Greg became instantly contrite. "I'm sorry, Carmen. I didn't mean to unload all this on you so soon. It's just—" He broke off and apologized again. "Sorry. We'll go now."

"No!" Carmen surprised herself as much as Greg with her outburst. Then she repeated it more calmly. "No. I'm not going anywhere until I've gotten an explanation."

He stared at her for a moment, then said quietly, "Okay, but we can't chance it out here. As I disconnected the Ear, the Humanoids might come along any time now to fix it."

Carmen saw what he was leading up to and refused emphatically. "I can't go in there! I absolutely cannot!"

"I understand." Greg kept calm. "The Humanoids have forbidden it. That's probably how they caught you in the first place, so I can't really blame you. Do you mind if I go in?"

Carmen's throat closed off. She shook her head, but she did mind. Terribly. She did not want Greg to be Removed as she had been. While it was true he held the answers to so many questions she had left unasked, there was another, troubling reason—but she couldn't put her finger on it.

Greg wasn't very long, pushing the button with a sureness born of long practice, and disappeared inside. Still, for Carmen, it was a very long wait. Questions had buzzed around in her head so persistently that at first she didn't notice the sheaf of papers he held in one hand. Then her eyes sharpened. Her Drawings! What was he doing with them? Without a word, he handed them over and Carmen looked at them one by one, only to drop the whole pile a moment later.

She clutched at the wall for support. An inarticulate sound rose in her throat that might have been a name. She blinked once, trying to clear away the image, but the array of pictures remained fanned out on the floor. The first nine were familiar scenes and Children of the Underground; the last four she couldn't remember ever committing to paper. They were completed drawings, each representing hours of work, and their subject matter was unmistakable, identical in detail down to that lone scar on the right temple. Greg.

"Are you okay?" Greg asked, moving forward to stand beside her.

Carmen's eyes never left the drawings. She stared at them for a long time, then reached into her pocket and withdrew a folded sheet of paper. Her Dream Drawing. She opened it and let it flutter to the ground as well.

CHAPTER SEVEN

Orange Sky?

Greg sucked in a breath. He looked from the Drawing to her accusingly. "You knew!"

"I know nothing!" Carmen said passionately, startling Greg with her vehemence. She startled herself as well and spoke in a calmer tone. "This is my Dream. I drew it before I ever saw you." She turned towards him almost pleadingly. "Am I mad?"

Greg made a funny sound in the back of his throat, half-laugh half-groan. She overrode it, in need of an answer. "Am I?" Her voice cracked.

His laughter stopped. "Of course you're not!" Greg's tone was gentle.

Carmen looked vastly relieved and her smile was dazzling. "The Dreams are often a sign of madness and I was—"

"Madness?" Greg was shocked. "Dreams have nothing to do with madness. Who ever gave you such an idea?" Greg asked angrily—not that there was much doubt. "The Humanoids, I suppose?" Carmen nodded and small sparks appeared in Greg's eyes. "The Humanoids are the mad ones for thinking they could ever keep us apart. The only thing they've succeeded in doing is putting us back to square one again—trying to get out of here."

Carmen withdrew a little at his words, her topaz eyes clouding over slightly. Greg cursed himself inwardly. He'd said the wrong thing. Again.

He sighed and began abruptly. "You said you wanted an explanation? Fine, you deserve one." He sat down, gesturing for Carmen to follow suit. "This might take a while. Comfortable?" She nodded. Greg paused, trying to get his thoughts in proper order. "First of all, you'd better know that I'm from the Overworld." This produced no reaction from Carmen other than a slight widening of her eyes and the thoughtful tilt to her head. Greg took a deep breath and plunged into the rest of the story, telling it as he remembered it.

He watched her face carefully the whole time, seeing the shock when he told her of his and Donald's fight and their Disobeying the Bell. Her cheeks went red at the story of their Choosing and she listened in silence up to the point when she was Removed.

"Well?" he said anxiously when he was through. "Does any of this ring a bell?"

Carmen shook her head sadly. "Your story has helped me understand a great many things which had been puzzling me since my Removal, things I have wanted very much to know. All the same—" she hesitated slightly, making eye contact, "—I do not think we should talk about it anymore. What you have told me about the Humanoids disturbs me greatly."

Greg's heart suddenly sank, anticipating her next words. "But you don't believe me, do you?" His voice was raw. He knew he was making too big of a thing out of this, but was unable to stop. "Whenever it comes right down to it, you'll choose the Humanoids over me every time, won't you?"

"I don't know you!" The words seemed torn from Carmen. She jumped up, clearly agitated. "Up until a few hours ago, I'd never seen you before in my life!"

"But the drawing—" Greg started.

Carmen turned very pale. "I told you," she said in a low voice, "it was from my Dream."

"Yeah, your Dream," Greg repeated. "You drew my face from the memory of one dream. Don't you see—"

"I don't want to *talk* about my Dream!" Carmen's voice broke. "I just don't want to talk about it anymore, okay?" She ended on what sounded suspiciously like a pleading note.

Greg looked into her eyes a long time, and saw the fear of madness that lay back of them. "Okay," he said quietly at last. He would have to be patient. "You win. I won't say anything more about it, unless you ask, and that's a promise."

Carmen looked at him warily. "Define *promise*."

A grin of relief spread over Greg's features and he felt himself relaxing. This he was used to. He helped her to her feet. "Well, a promise is,..." he began to explain as they started walking back to the Exercise Room where the rest of the Children were. Greg unplugged the Ear on the way.

For a few days they talked mostly of Project and other Underground matters. Greg still kept near her for he had an irrational fear of the Humanoids coming and Removing Carmen all over again when his back was turned. He managed to coax some laughter out of her and even from Donald who sat on the other side of them. Over and above the need to escape, it became his goal in life to bring the golden light back into Carmen's eyes.

One favourite way was to insult the Food. First, he would poke at it, then slowly bring it up to his lips and make horrible faces while he ate. The taste of the food never varied: it was totally bland and doughy to chew on. Then one day, much to Greg's surprise, there was a slight salty taste to it.

"Well, what do you know?" he exclaimed. "There's actually some flavour in the food for a change!"

"It's probably the radioactivites," Carmen remarked innocently, putting her spoon to her mouth.

Greg nearly choked. "The what?" he sputtered.

Carmen favoured him with a half-angry, half-amused look. "You weren't listening when I told you about my Project were you? The radioactivites are necessary. They've been injected into the Food in small quantities."

"Necessary?" Greg's interest sharpened. "Necessary for what?"

Carmen shrugged. She knew what radioactivites did, but the technical explanation required more time than they were allowed and didn't give much of an answer anyway. Not the one Greg wanted. Carmen was quickly beginning to learn that when Greg asked a question he wanted cause and effect more than anything else; and cause was something the Humanoids were short on. She satisfied him by replying with another question. "Would you rather wear a protective mask at all times?" That had been the only other solution proposed by the Humanoids.

Greg frowned and dropped the subject. Carmen noticed, with some amusement, that while he didn't eat any more of his Food, he downed his Drink without difficulty. She managed to refrain from pointing out that the radioactivites were just as likely, if not more likely, to be in the Drink as the Food. They would certainly be able to dissolve in larger quantities.

Some of the other compounds she made up in the next few days of Project were not so easily administered. They reacted badly with the nutrient and had to be injected directly. With a needle.

When the announcement was made that everyone *must* have them and that the shots were scheduled instead of Project, more people than just Greg were concerned. In the past, the only thing that had been allowed to interrupt Project was the Choosing. This worried Carmen more than she was willing to admit. Strange things were beginning to happen in the Underground and they included Greg's whole presence there. It was obvious the Children were being prepared for something. But for what?

Carmen and those of the Medical Project received their shots first. There were no side effects, not known ones anyway. Certainly no time was wasted watching for them; there were others to be treated as well.

Instead of doing the actual administering, Carmen found herself running the Analyzer to determine what each individual needed and in what quantities. In all, that meant thirty-five Children to be Analyzed with no less than four scans to be recorded per person. It added up to quite a bit of work, more than Carmen could ever recall doing on any one Project. She wondered at Belle's unfailing energy as the day wore on.

"Aren't you tired?" Carmen asked her.

Belle paused only fractionally. "No," she answered and drew a clear solution into her syringe.

Greg was patient number thirty-three. The number three sounded familiar somehow, but Carmen was given no time to dwell upon it. She correctly positioned Greg under the ray and flipped a few switches. Greg looked a little nervous. Instead of psychosoothing him as she had been taught, Carmen just joked with him like they usually did at lunch time. She knew instinctively that Greg would not appreciate being given the recommended treatment.

The Analyzer spewed out the first of its reports, and Carmen went to get it. She read it in silence, a frown spreading over her face.

"What is it?" Greg asked immediately.

"It's very strange," Carmen murmured without looking up.

She did not mean to be cryptic, but Greg let loose a sigh of impatience and came to peek over her shoulder. "Strange is the word for it, all right! How on earth you can make any sense out of that is beyond me."

But Carmen was too anxious to react to the backhanded compliment. "Look!" she commanded, tapping the paper. "You already have a 35 percent viosterol reading. You don't need the treatment."

"Fine with me." Greg resumed his spot under the Analyzer's particle ray. "Now then—"

Another report slid out and Carmen walked over to read it, ignoring Greg. She wasn't sure she wanted to look. She stared at it awhile.

"So?" Greg's voice had a smile to it, one she could almost see. "Do I take it that I've avoided yet another needle?"

"No." Carmen's voice was troubled. "But your percentage is a lot higher than everyone else's. It's 5 percent."

Greg shrugged. "Doesn't sound so high to me."

Carmen's voice was dry when she replied. "It is when you consider mine was .002 percent."

"Oh," said a rather subdued Greg. There wasn't much else he could say.

The last two tests both came out positive—no needles. Greg tried to make a joke out of it, but Carmen wasn't biting. Long after the day was over, she was still trying to puzzle it out. It was almost as if he already had been given the treatments sometime in the past and just didn't remember them. On that note Carmen fell asleep.

The next morning, Greg was uncharacteristically silent throughout most of Meal A. His whole expression was one of distance and Carmen fell silent herself, studying him and worrying. Finally, just before the Bell rang, he turned and asked, "Carmen, the reading that I got 5 percent on and you got .002 percent, what was it for? And how much does one need in order to skip getting the shot?"

Carmen sought to conceal her surprise. "It was an Ultra-indigo reading. Twenty-seven percent is needed."

"Indigo? Not violet?" Worry lines cut into Greg's forehead.

Carmen shook her head. She wanted to ask what he meant, but the C-chime went and they had to go. Once they were actually in the Assembly Room all thought of Greg's high readings went out of her mind. Something was in the wind for today.

For one thing, there was an unusual number of Humanoids present. And after the Progress Reports had been given, a dozen or so blue-jumpsuited Factors filed in. Except for two, they were all known to Carmen. Originally they had been part of the Children, but they had advanced a level as their Factor Groups filled up. It was rarely, if ever, that their paths crossed.

Her attention was pulled back to the front by the astonishing request to remain seated and the announcement that all Projects be postponed that day.

Ripples of shock went through the Children. No such change in scheduling had ever been given before. Carmen glanced over at Greg and found him grim and silent. A nameless feeling of unease crawled over her.

"Children." The Humanoid at the front held up a hand and all talk immediately ceased. "You have lived in the Underground all your lives, as did your Factors before you. But, as you know, it was not always so. Some of your Factors Squared and all of your Factors Cubed came from a different place—the Overworld."

The Humanoid paused briefly, allowing time for the absorption of the material. Its impersonal eyes raked through the crowd, as if searching for some kind of reaction. After they passed over her, Carmen discovered that she had been holding her breath. She let it out in a gush, unsure of her reasons for holding it in the first place. Her inborn curiosity kept her ears attuned to what the Humanoid was saying.

"The Overworld was a place of much confusion and its People were prone to panic. They feared the very things that were trying to help them. Some of the People would promote feelings of violence throughout the Overworld.

"As an act of prevention, they were Removed to a safe place. The Underground. These were your Factors Cubed."

A collective gasp went up. Carmen felt within her a deep sense of shame. Her Factors Cubed: malcontents, promoters of violence!

The Humanoid's next words banished her thoughts. "Over time, the Underground has grown crowded and Choosings harder. This is true of all the Undergrounds in the world. The need for an Underground has now passed. It has been decided that as soon as your Preparation has been completed, the ascent into the Overworld will begin."

A surge of excitement shot through Carmen. The Overworld! Greg's Overworld! She turned to him in excitement, eyes glowing. Although she hadn't admitted it to Greg, his story of the Overworld had fascinated her. Ever since her Removal, she had been looking at the

Underground with different eyes. She no longer felt comfortable around the Humanoids or even most of the Children.

"You won't have to escape now!" she told Greg. It wasn't until the words were said that she realized exactly how great that relief was. Before, if Greg had been caught trying to go to the Overworld, he would have been Removed and Carmen did not want that to happen. Not for anything.

"No, I won't have to escape now, will I?" Greg said. There was a strange note to his voice that made Carmen look at him more closely.

"Aren't you happy?" Her own voice was troubled.

For her sake, Greg tried to smile. "Of course. I want to go to the Overworld. I want to show it to you. But—" he hesitated, unsure of how Carmen would take his words, "—I don't trust the Humanoids. The whole thing's too easy."

Just then the Humanoids started up the first of the three-dimensional models on the hologrammer and Greg lapsed back into moody silence.

"Drawn to a scale of 1:1,500,000, this is *The Surface of The Earth.*"

Carmen nodded along with the others. The central layers of it they had, of course, already studied along with the laws of gravity and air pressure that went with it .

"The Overworld has a multitude of natural phenomena that the Underground lacks." The holoshow images began to flash all around them, almost real enough to touch—so real, in fact, that Carmen caught herself flinching as a forked rod of light cut seemingly too close to her.

"They fit into a number of different categories. The first is *Sky.*" The whole ceiling took on an orange, almost red colour. "This is the uppermost layer of the Overworld. It is unpurified and consists of 18 percent oxygen, 7 percent carbon dioxide and 74 percent nitrogen."

Carmen tilted her head to one side. That left 1 percent. It was probably of the same mixture the 4 percent unpure air she was breathing right now. The figure for nitrogen, however, far exceeded the 52 percent in the Underground. Imagine, 74 percent nitrogen! It boggled the mind.

And that, Carmen was quick to realize, was only the beginning. There were gray-green masses of water vapour called *Clouds* that poured water in the form of droplets to earth and the all-important *Sun* that was really a great ball of gas and fire. The thing called *The Moon* was less important and barely mentioned as the planet's satellite and visible only at night. And the phenomenon that intrigued Carmen the most, the great bands of colour that appeared with the rain, was not defined at all. Only the principle of the circulation of air was the same in both worlds; though up above, Carmen learned, moving air was capable of extremely high speeds. *Winds*.

Also, there was the strange concept of hot versus cold instead of just one even temperature. This seemed essentially impractical to Carmen, but if that was the way things were....

The next category was of *The Sea*. The tides and waves that ruled it were essentially logical; the only thing Carmen had trouble comprehending was the immense size of it. Almost three-quarters of a 12,756-kilometre diameter planet. The last time Carmen had felt so awed was when the specimen under her microscope had seemed to stare back at her and she had realized just how big she must look to it.

She mentioned this to Greg, saying, "It seems almost unbelievable. I used to wonder if the Overworld really existed or if it was just a story."

"Of course it exists!" Greg's voice was so loud and so fierce that Carmen could not help but look askance at him.

The words set off a weird chain of reaction inside of her, only to stop one link short. It left her groping for more. She turned to Greg, at a loss to explain, yet wanting to share the feeling.

He seemed to understand and gave her hand a squeeze. "*Déjà vu*. That which has already been seen."

Carmen hadn't really seen anything, but she thought she knew what he meant. It was like going back in time, she decided, and having the same thing happen all over again. It unnerved her, raising goosebumps on her arms.

By now they had advanced to *The Land and Its Inhabitants*. The in-depth nature of the presentation supplied everything that Carmen hungered after. She was held fascinated. Greg, on the other hand, grew increasingly restless as the show wore on, until Carmen at last turned to him and whispered, "What's the matter?"

But he just shook his head and whispered, "Later." Mystified, Carmen went back to watching and was soon caught up in the display. Great masses of rock, called *Mountains,* were being pushed up as two continental plates collided. The forces involved were tremendous and had taken thousands of lifetimes.

The mountain images faded into a display of five bodies of water called *The Great Lakes* which were fresh water and, for that reason, had not been included in the Sea category. "It is here," the Humanoid announced, "that we will settle." The dizzying aerial view of the Lakes became more focussed, grew nearer until the audience seemed to be skimming past along the deserted lakeshore.

A low rumbling began in the distance, reminding Carmen of the phenomenon called *Thunder.* It grew louder until they were suddenly faced with a virtual wall of water that rushed over a U-shaped cliff and straight down, raising up clouds of water vapour at the bottom. *"Niagara Falls,"* the Humanoid instructed.

Beside her, Greg made a made a silent, involuntary movement that drew Carmen's attention to him. His face was very pale, though still not as ivory-toned as the rest of the Children. It was not a time when talk was permissible so she reached for his hand instead.

His eyes did not move from the scene around them, but she noticed his pupils looked somehow bigger in the green of his eye. He squeezed her hand very hard.

They took a break for Meal B shortly afterwards, but still Greg said nothing, not even pretending to eat his Food today. In mute protest Carmen didn't touch hers either, just looked at him and waited. He began abruptly, "Carmen, I'm scared." And he was. His hands were practically icy, something he couldn't remember ever happening before. When Carmen had been Removed, he had first his anger and then Donald's assurances to protect him from this awful, numbing fear. "That's not the Overworld they've been showing us."

Carmen looked uncomprehending and he laughed. Or tried to. The only thing that came out was a horrible, choking sound. "At least not the Overworld I lived in. My Overworld has a blue sky, not an orange one. It's a small enough quibble, to be sure. The Humanoids might simply have made a mistake, but I doubt it." Greg took a sip of Drink to ease the lump in his throat.

"And then there's the amount of radiation in the air. You said I had 5 percent ultra-indigo, but they wanted 27 percent. Why? There's not much point in giving everyone needles for nothing." Greg thumped the table for emphasis. Heads turned and he paused to glare them all back down before starting again.

"It must be some kind of protection," mused Carmen, "but against what?"

"And then the biggie," continued Greg. "Where are the people? Remember those river fronts we skimmed by?" Carmen nodded. "Last year, or whenever I was last there, there were condos and restaurants all along that river. There's supposed to be a whole city there, and I didn't see so much as rubble! I thought I must have gotten my rivers confused until I saw Niagara Falls. That's one place that's always swarming with people no matter what the season."

"Maybe they were just away for the day," Carmen suggested.

Greg's smile was bitter. "I'm afraid you don't understand, Carmen. This was a city, with hundreds of thousands of people and thousands of buildings to live and work in. A city can't just up and disappear without a trace. No," said Greg with absolute conviction, "something's happened out there to make the Overworld like this and it's nothing good. Oh, Carmen!" He turned to her with agonized eyes. "My whole family's up there. Mom and Dad and Lucy." He could say no more.

Carmen put her hands on his shoulder, instinctively offering the comfort he needed. When she did speak, it was reassuringly logical. "We're jumping to conclusions, taking appearances to mean facts. Just because the images we were shown do not include people, does not mean the city doesn't exist. Who knows?" she tried to speak lightly. "*People* might be our next category."

"Maybe." Greg forced a smile and even attempted to eat some of his Food. Most of its heat was gone and after a couple of mouthfuls he laid down his spoon. He felt calmer now. As always, talking to Carmen about it had helped. Although he could tell she did not completely understand, she understood more than anyone else. She always would.

The C-chime went and they filed back to the Assembly Room. But the next category was much more broad, that of *Space and the Whole Universe Beyond Earth.* Although relatively little was known about the subject, the holographic display took up the whole afternoon by dazzling them with special effects. Then, the machine clicked off and a Humanoid took the floor once again. "Are there any questions?"

There were, and Carmen was among those who raised a hand. "Don't!" Greg grabbed it and pulled it down, but not in time. The Humanoid's eyes flashed in their direction. "Yes, Carmen?"

And Carmen, who had been about to ask about the people, quickly substituted a question about the bands of colour instead. They turned out to be something called a *Rainbow* caused by the refraction of sunlight through quintillions of water droplets. Carmen nodded as if satisfied. When the Humanoid went on to the next person, Carmen glanced at Greg curiously.

He appeared to be relieved. "Boy, you scared me for a minute there! I thought for sure you'd ask about the people."

"I was going to," Carmen admitted. "Why didn't you want me to?"

"The Humanoids would have gotten too suspicious. They watch us all the time as it is," Greg explained in a whisper. "I have the feeling that if either of us makes one more misstep, that's it. End of line."

Carmen fought down a shiver. She waited until Meal C to talk under the covering noise of the Children eating. "What are we going to do?" she asked, consciously allying herself against the Humanoids.

"The unexpected." A dangerous spark appeared in Greg's green eyes. The Humanoids weren't used to dealing with Overworlders like himself and therein lay his advantage. "The fact that we're still being prepared gives us a little extra time. Whatever they're planning on doing to the Overworld might not have already taken place. We can still save the world," he grinned crookedly, "providing, of course, that we escape this rat trap first."

"Of course," Carmen agreed, frowning at his grin. "That would be a priority." Greg shot her a funny look, but she continued. "We need more information. We need to know exactly what's going to happen up there." Information, she had been taught as a child, was vital. "And since we can't risk asking for it ourselves, we're going to need help."

"Who? Donald! Of course!" Greg answered his own question and beamed at Carmen. "I'll ask him."

For some reason, Carmen found herself rather puzzled by his enthusiasm. She didn't know why. She had been about to suggest Donald herself, but somehow she had expected a different reaction from Greg. "Didn't you fight with Donald?" she asked inquisitively.

Greg grinned wider. "Sure did! Too bad the Humanoids interrupted us."

Carmen gave up then. She had always thought violence promoted bad feelings, not friendships. There was a lot yet she had to learn about the Overworld.

The C-chime went and it was decided that Greg would explain the whole thing to Donald during his next Tri-Dynamics Project. Greg would have preferred to tell him now when they had the spare time, but Donald was deep in conversation with Ilka and probably wouldn't appreciate the interruption. And, as Greg recalled, he and Donald were on the same shift later that day.

After dropping off Carmen at Laser Healing, Greg walked along towards Tri-Dynamics at a fast pace. He caught a glimpse of Donald up ahead and sped up, manoeuvering his way through traffic with ease. "Hey, Donald," he said lightly, tapping him on the shoulder.

There was time only for Donald to turn and telegraph him a silent alert, before two Humanoids stepped in on Greg from either side of the doorway and closed their hands over his wrists.

Instinctively, Greg made a leap for freedom, but the steel hands held him fast. In a moment it was all over. A small sting, no more than a pinprick, and everything was suddenly in blurry, slow motion. The world spun ever-blacker before Greg's eyes. The last thing he heard was the soothing voice of the Humanoids saying, "We will not hurt you. We will not—"

CHAPTER EIGHT

Escape

Laser Healing Project had just started and Carmen was awaiting her turn at precision cutting with her hand laser when she heard the footsteps. They were the familiar tromp, tromp of the Humanoids and it was largely a matter of luck that made Carmen glance out the doorway at them. It took no more than a second for the situation to become clear to her. Two shining Humanoids were carrying Greg, *her* Greg, away. Greg's eyes were closed and his body limp in their arms.

Carmen screamed. Long and loud.

As a strategic move, it could hardly have been better. The Children around the Humanoids froze, impeding motion, and it spurred Carmen into action herself.

Of their own volition Carmen's legs speeded up into a blur. She was running, on her toes as Greg had taught her, but was aware only of the need to stop the Humanoids.

She threw herself at their legs, unbalancing them so that Greg slid out of their arms, unconscious, to the floor. "Greg!" If Carmen had ever had any doubts about how she felt about Greg, they were banished in that instant. She knelt down beside him, feeling tears prick at the back of her eyes.

"Move away." The Humanoids, no longer off-balance, came forward arms outstretched.

"No!" The word was explosive coming from someone Carmen's size. She was on her feet in an instant, her whole attitude one of a tigress at bay. Her golden eyes were ablaze with anger. "You stay away from him! Hear me? Get away!" she shouted.

"He is in need of our help." The words were meant to be soothing, but Carmen didn't find them so. She, who had always thought of violence with distaste, was ready to attack at the slightest movement.

"You are taking him away from me! But I won't let you do it." Carmen did not know exactly how she knew this, but at the moment it did not matter. She would not let them take Greg away from her. Not again. The words were tacked on as an afterthought.

The Humanoid on the right took a step forward. "You're upset, Carmen. We can help that, too."

Carmen shook her head fiercely. They were trying to trick her. But while she argued with one, the other crept up behind her. Her voice rose to a shriek. "I'm warning you, get away!" But they didn't heed her, and continued to walk closer. Too close.

Desperately, without pausing to think, Carmen raised the hand laser and fired at the closest one. The verdeocrystal inside shot out a thin, green beam that sliced the Humanoid in half. The second Humanoid paused, its lights blinking in confusion. "Stop that, Carmen—" it started to say, its voice neither higher pitched nor louder than before. Carmen swung her laser blindly towards the noise and carved the Humanoid's legs out from under it. It fell face down on the floor, still repeating, "Stop that, Carmen. Stop that—" Another swipe with the laser and that noise stopped as well. A viscous, red liquid welled up around the cut parts and dripped onto the floor.

Dazed, Carmen switched off the laser and looked up. The Children were staring at her. Most of them had moved far over to the sides to avoid being hit. None spoke so much as a word. There were no other Humanoids, not yet anyway. They would be coming. For a moment Carmen almost gave up and dropped her laser. She was genuinely horrified at what she had done. But another look at Greg's still figure stopped her. She couldn't let them take Greg!

She had to think. Carmen's mind suddenly became very clear and with the clear came a calmness of which she hadn't known she was capable. She spoke quietly, in her best psychosoothe, "All of you go back to your Projects.

You'll be safe there. All of you go back to your Projects." Sluggishly at first, the Children began to move, then, out of habit, they formed orderly lines and filed in—all without a word passing their lips.

Carmen surveyed Greg's bulk. He was too heavy for her to carry all by herself; she would need help. "Donald," Carmen whispered, then said it louder, "Donald!" The lines of Children froze, then stirred as Donald stepped forward, and quietly proceeded again.

"Help me carry him." Carmen's voice was calm, but her eyes pleaded. She could feel her pulse pounding in her throat. They had to get out of here. *Now.* Before more Humanoids came.

To her relief Donald made no protest, his face pale and set as he grabbed onto Greg's ankles.

"Wait," Carmen said. The tunnel that Greg had told her about was just around the corner. If she could just take him there and hide him.... But first there was the problem of the Eyes. With the laser, she melted the two that were on the way, and then two more further down, so the trail wouldn't lead exactly to the tunnel.

She ran back to where Donald and Greg were and picked him up under the shoulders. He was quite heavy for someone who was unaccustomed to carrying anything heavier than a Food Tray. Carmen was panting by the time they made it around the corner. "Stop," she told Donald and leaned Greg's upper body against the wall. He tipped over, but she didn't have time to straighten him. In her mind, she could already hear the approaching tread of Humanoid feet.

Carmen tried to open the secret panel in the same way that Greg had, but when a light touch failed, she pounded on it frantically. When it did open, she nearly fell inside. "Come on!" she commanded, manoeuvering Greg's head and shoulders through the opening. But Donald balked.

"I can't go in there!" he protested.

"Oh yes, you can!" Carmen kept walking backwards with Greg's body, her voice hoarse with fear. Donald couldn't cop out on her now! He couldn't! "We can't let the Humanoids find us now!" Finally her urgency pulled him in. They paused only to slide the door shut after them. "Come on!" The passageway was a narrow one and Carmen had to twist her head tightly in order to see where they were going.

At one point they passed an Eye. Fortunately, a sheet of white paper hung in front of it, taped to the ceiling. The view it would give would look the same as the blank white wall opposite it. Exhaling a sigh of relief, Carmen thought she knew who to thank for that.

The tunnel ended in an empty room, totally empty except for her pile of Drawings and materials. Ever so gently, Carmen lowered Greg's head to the floor. Hovering over him, she loosened the jumpsuit around his throat and arranged his arms down by his sides.

"Is this place safe? I mean, to talk?" Donald stared nervously at the four stark walls around them, searching for Ears.

"Absolutely. Did Greg get a chance to tell you about the Overworld?"

Donald frowned. "No, he came up behind me just as I was going into Project. I tried to warn him about the Humanoids, but there wasn't time. What about the Overworld?" Donald asked. Carmen wasn't the only one to have inherited the trait of curiosity.

Carmen explained it to him, using the differences between his Analyzer tests and Greg's as an example. When she was done, Donald was beginning to look concerned. "Billions of people?" he questioned.

Carmen shrugged. She couldn't imagine it either. "That's what Greg said."

"Carmen?" The voice was weak, but unmistakable. It was Greg.

"Yes?" Carmen bent over him, cradling his head on her lap. She took his pulse with deft fingers. Greg's green eyes fluttered open and he looked up at her trying to focus.

"What happened?" Greg whispered, peeking up at her from under one half-closed eyelid.

"The Humanoids drugged you, but you should be back to normal in a half an hour."

"I know that." The impatient note in Greg's voice made Carmen smile in relief. He was going to be okay. "I meant, what am I doing here? If the Humanoids drugged me, why aren't I with them?"

Carmen suddenly blushed, and it was left for Donald to answer in a dry voice. "Carmen saw you being taken away and cut the Humanoids to pieces with her laser. She couldn't lift you by herself, which explains why I'm here."

Greg's head swung her way again. "Is that true, Carmen?" He sounded shocked and maybe a little amused. "You shot them?"

"Yes," she admitted quietly. It was not something she was particularly proud of, but there had been no other option. Her eyes darkened. "They were going to take you away."

Greg's hand came up to touch her hair. "My heroine," he said half-jokingly, then more seriously, "Thank you, Carmen."

Carmen kept absolutely still until his hand dropped. She did not smile, but her eyes glowed.

Greg pulled himself into a sitting position. A smile played across his face. "You really shot them?" Carmen nodded again, and he laughed. "Serves them right. I just wish I'd been there to see it."

Donald's mouth twitched as well. "It was well worth seeing."

Carmen studied them both in amazement. It was the worst thing that had ever happened to her and they were both laughing. Unbelievable. "What about the other Humanoids?" she asked abruptly. "Once they realize that both Donald and I knew of this room, it's the first place they'll look."

"Donald?" Greg raised an eyebrow. "I thought you told me that nobody knew of this room but yourself."

"Donald was Removed for it," Carmen explained briefly. "He didn't remember finding it after that."

"You did." Greg's tone was blunt.

Carmen smiled. "Yes, but I knew of it before I met you. And they only erased my memory from that point on and set up a mental block."

"That's what I got Removed for?" Donald interrupted incredulously. "Just for finding this place?"

"Yes," Carmen said, somewhat impatiently. "That's what I said. Now what are we going to do about the Humanoids?"

"Wait," Greg held up a hand. "Donald's got a point there. If you were both Removed for the same thing, there must obviously be something important about this place."

"Like what?" Carmen looked around it quickly. The walls were white as were the floors, and that was really all there was to it. Just an empty room.

"Like maybe an exit." Greg was up on his feet in seconds. "Check the corners," he instructed them. Catching on to his excitement, Carmen obeyed and began poking and pounding for a secret button. A few minutes later there was a yell from Greg. "Jackpot!"

They all stared into the opening in the wall. The passageway was gray, crumbly concrete and led upward, not on a gentle slant, but in a series of short ninety-degree bumps. "Stairs," Greg breathed the word as if it were sacred and ran up a half a dozen or so. "Come on, what are you waiting for?"

Hesitantly, Carmen stepped through the door and lifted first one foot and then the other, till she was standing about twenty centimetres up.

But Donald hung back. "This goes to the Overworld?" he asked cautiously.

"How would I know?" Greg shot back impatiently. "That's what we're going to find out. Now are you coming or aren't you?"

Donald shook his head decisively. "No, I'm not. I'd like to—" his eyes pleaded for understanding, "—but I can't go. Not without Ilka."

Carmen's stomach untensed itself and she nodded. "I see. But what about the Humanoids? They'll probably Remove you," she pointed out practically.

"Don't worry about me," Donald's tone was calm. "I'll just tell them that you threatened to cut me in half if I didn't do what you said. And I'm not repairable."

There was an awkward pause before Greg came back down and held out his hand to Donald. Donald raised an eyebrow and shook the proffered hand. He nodded when Greg said, "We'll be back. And all the Children will be able to come to the Overworld on their own terms."

An unexplained lump came into Carmen's throat making speech difficult. Still, she tried. "I wish you were coming with us, Donald. Good-bye."

When Donald disappeared back the way they had come, Greg turned towards the stairs, looking amused when he saw Carmen's attempt to climb them. "No, no, like this," he demonstrated. "See? No more than one foot has to touch each step, sometimes not even that."

Carmen tried it again and this time found it easier. Less effort anyway.

There was a yell from down the other end of the corridor, startling Carmen so much that she stepped backwards and fell down the few steps she had climbed. The yell had been Donald's, but the steady footsteps that followed were definitely Humanoid.

Greg took one peek out of the doorway and whirled, pulling Carmen to her feet none too gently. "They're coming," he told her tersely. "Go!" He pointed up the staircase.

He turned his attention towards closing the door and wasted precious seconds looking for a way to secure it. There was none. They'd just have to make a run for it. He looked up astonished to see Carmen was still with him.

"What are you waiting for?" He didn't wait for an answer, just grabbed her hand and ran.

There was only one way to go: up. After the first flight of stairs, the hall twisted a little, heading off to the right and then left before going up again. Together they pounded up countless stairs before, breathless and shiny-eyed, Carmen motioned for a stop. His own breath was coming in gasps too big to talk around so Greg just nodded, ready to run again the moment the Humanoids got too close.

But the expected footsteps never came. Carmen finally broke their silence. "They're not coming."

A wild babble of protest rose inside Greg. The Humanoids had been chasing them. He had not imagined those precise footsteps.

"No," Carmen repeated, "they're not." Her breathing had slowed to a more manageable rate now, but she still had trouble talking. "Why should they? We've caused them nothing but trouble. They're ... probably saying good riddance right now." Her sides shook with silent laughter and tears of mirth formed in her eyes. "Maybe they were planning on dumping us in the Overworld anyway!"

Greg didn't find it very funny at all. He thought of the needle he had taken in the arm and of their headlong bolt up the stairs. "Why didn't you tell me?" he asked, slightly disgruntled.

Carmen sobered immediately. "Because I might have been wrong."

This was so true that Greg subsided without another word. They had both done what was right. The Humanoids were not to be trusted.

The unwelcome thought came to Greg that, rather than come up behind them, the Humanoids could very well be waiting for them at the top en masse. Carmen had a laser, it was true, but that just might make the Humanoids decide to kill instead of capture them. The possibility was enough to jerk Greg to his feet.

"What is it?" Carmen asked immediately.

Greg hesitated, then decided it wasn't necessary that she know. He helped her to her feet, his old carefree grin slipping into place. "Coming? The Overworld can't be too far away now."

Carmen's answer was just as lighthearted, but with the ring of truth behind it. "I would follow you anywhere."

As long as she didn't follow him to her death, thought Greg gloomily. He kept his eyes open and his ears trained for the slightest sound.

Sure enough, a few flights later, Greg was positive he could hear something over and above the steady hum that characterized the Underground. The stairs ended at a white door six steps above. Greg, still climbing, whispered in Carmen's ear. "Stay here while I open the door. Get your laser ready in case there are Humanoids."

Carmen nodded, her face pale but determined.

Rather than tip off the Humanoids by walking any differently, Greg climbed the remaining steps at the same rate as his previous pace. Then, two steps from the top, he yanked the door open, flattening himself against the opposite wall so Carmen would have a clear view.

With a deafening boom, the door rebounded off the wall, swinging closed again, but not before Greg got a look inside—at nothing. There were no Humanoids.

Grinning foolishly, Greg reopened the door and held it for Carmen. "The coast is clear."

As well as being clear, it appeared they had reached the last of the stairs. A corridor slanted off to one side. The diagonal deviation was so different from the usual right-angle corners of the Underground that Greg couldn't help but feel they were nearing the end of the road. He found himself walking faster towards the noises.

Smells were beginning to reach them now. Greg welcomed them all, even the musty smell of damp earth. He'd been too long in the Underground, shut in by walls where everything was super-clean. He wanted to be a part of the city again, to feel the sting of wind on his face, the grit underfoot. So many things.

The hall gave way to an opening which led to a large tunnel. It was darker here and Carmen's grip on his hand tightened. Greg returned the squeeze. "We'll be in the light again soon." The dark didn't frighten him. One of the first things he had found out about, and hated, in the Underground was the permanent presence of light, be it morning, noon or night.

Something small scurried across the floor near their feet and she jumped, hanging back. Protectively, Greg slowed down to more her pace. If the Underground had panicked him when he first discovered he was trapped there, how was Carmen going to feel when confronted with a whole new world? The Humanoid presentations had given her a hint of things to come, but they were hardly anything to go on.

A heavy sound rumbled overhead. Carmen stopped dead, refusing to budge. "What is it? I can't see!"

Quite unlike himself, Greg didn't try to kid her out of it, saying simply, "I'm right here, Carmen. The city may make a lot of noises, but it doesn't often bite. We can go as slow as you like."

"I'm okay." Carmen's voice was so soft that Greg had to stop breathing to hear her.

A sudden flash of memory made Greg pull her forward. "I think we might be in an old subway tunnel." He sensed Carmen's puzzlement and hastened to explain. "It was a mode of travel our ancestors used. That was before the Techno Age, of course. They were probably just going out of use when the Underground was built."

But Carmen was only mildly interested in this. "How soon," she asked, "how soon before we reach the top?" Greg was about to say he didn't know, but just then his fingers, which had been trailing along the wall, encountered a corner. Around it, the darkness lightened, lending a glitter to her eyes that might have been either excitement or fear—or perhaps a little of both.

Anticipation filled Greg as well, quickening his stride. "Not long now." The rumbling was definitely louder now and the light brighter. Carmen's eyes met his and in unspoken agreement they began to run, confidently and without the desperation of before.

The light was in the outline of a door, leaking out through the cracks. For the first time, Greg could see the dust and age of the place. The ceiling was low and cobwebbed. Two parallel tracks of rusting steel lay near their feet. As a form of transportation it left something to be desired and Greg could see why it was called a subway rather than a highway. From behind the door, the noises of the street came through almost loudly enough to be right beside them.

Carmen was openly trembling and it took Greg a moment longer than usual to open the door.

The air was the first thing. Cold, and with the faint taint that had been missing in the Underground. Greg breathed in deep lungfuls of it. The Overworld! Greg's eyes drank in the sight of domed and irregularly shaped buildings (no more ninety-degree angles!) plus a whole panorama of colour and movement. And people! Greg was very relieved to see people walking the streets and peering down from glass buildings. His glance followed a needle-shaped green tower up until it reached the sky. Partly cloudy sky. Greg's eyes searched frantically for a glimpse of blue between the clouds. It wasn't until he'd reassured himself—twice—that the sky was really blue and not orange that he allowed himself to turn and watch Carmen's reaction.

Her eyes were very wide despite the undoubted brightness of the sun burning down on them. It was rather hot and Greg decided with relief that it must be summer, not winter as he had feared. Ice and snow would have proven even more of a culture shock to Carmen. Their jumpsuits would hardly have been adequate protection against the cold.

As it was, she had yet to move from the slight shelter offered her by the doorway and Greg's shoulder. For the longest time she simply stood and stared, saying in awe, "It really can't compare, can it?"

Greg thought back to the polished, but somehow dull Underground. "No," he agreed, and a hint of pride showed in his voice. "It really can't."

"So," Carmen said after a moment's silence, "where do we go from here?" She was trying to hide it, but some of her nervousness had returned.

"Home," Greg replied with no hesitation whatsoever. It was amazing the strength of feeling carried by that one little word.

"*Home*," Carmen repeated as if learning a lesson. But she was not gazing at the scene around her. She was looking at him.

CHAPTER NINE

The Grand Overseer

"Which way do we go now?" The gaze that Carmen turned on Greg was totally trusting. "How far is it to Home?" She was slightly disconcerted to see him laugh as if her words amused him.

His green eyes twinkled. "I'm afraid, Carmen, it's not quite as easy as all that. The city isn't some place that you know like the back of your hand. It's big, really big, and I don't even know where we are right now."

Being born to the Underground, Carmen had no real idea how of big *really big* was, but she could vaguely recall Greg once saying something about billions of people. The Children numbered only thirty-nine and the Humanoids a scant dozen. The first traces of panic began to ripple through her.

Fortunately, Greg recognized her growing fear. "Hey, relax! I'm a city boy. Just give me a street sign on a major artery and we're away to the races." He began to look around.

Carmen had trouble following exactly what he was talking about, but the confidence behind his words reassured her. This was his territory just as the Underground had been hers.

They came to a street called Queeneast and the news made Greg grin. "Home's this way. It's not too far." Carmen smiled back at him and followed. She did not even attempt to remember all the twists and turns in their trail; there were other things to look at.

There was blue Sky, not orange as the Humanoids had said. Tall buildings of varying shapes towered over her. Carmen stumbled several times, craning her neck to see their tops. Strange clear-plastic craft zipped along the streets, no more than a metre above the ground, while others stayed still and were responsible for the rumbling noises. After about the third rumble, the craft would shoot straight up in the air, come even with a building and people would disembark and others would crowd in. "How do you like the L-Vates?" asked Greg.

"Mmm," said Carmen politely. Although the lofty buildings were spotless and shiny, the streets were not. The Overworld was not a clean place like the Underground and Carmen wrinkled her nose in faint distaste.

But best, and most fascinating of all, were the people. All kinds of people, not just Children, and all dressed differently, no two kinds alike. Even the white jumpsuits that Carmen and Greg wore did not look too out of place although Greg fit in more than she did, moving with the crowds as if he had been born to them. Which, of course, she realized with a jolt, he had.

There were other pedestrians on the streets with them, and unlike the Underground, there were no white lines to divide them. Several of the people's faces interested her in particular and she turned to look after them as they passed by. Greg had to pull at her arm twice to get her back on the road. How she would have loved to have the time and tools to draw them! She smiled suddenly, brilliantly.

Greg pointed out a sign which said Woodbinary. "Come on! We're getting close." Greg's voice was impatient, but excited as well. They were nearing their destination. Home. Carmen tore her eyes away from the couple she had been watching and hurried. Greg was already several paces ahead of her. Had he not stopped, Carmen could easily have lost him to the crowd. Her heart knocked up against her ribs at the thought; from then on, Carmen took extra care not to lag behind. The Overworld might be interesting, but she had little doubt that it could become dangerous as well.

"Here we are." He pointed proudly to a square building labelled 100 Kippendavie Towers. Greg's tone held such satisfaction that Carmen couldn't help but glance at him. What was this Home that meant so much to him?

The building didn't look much different to her than any of the other ones in the Overworld. What set Home apart?

Greg tapped an access code into a built-in keyterm next to the door. But instead of the door opening, a buzzer sounded rudely. INVALID CODE, the thirty-by-thirty centimetre screen read.

"Have they moved or what?" growled Greg. "Help me look for Matheson." Carmen couldn't help but notice that the Homes were not assigned in alphabetical order. She wanted to ask about this inefficiency, but Greg had an intense expression on his face so she decided to wait.

A moment later he found it, his finger stabbing the board. "There it is! Apartment 3012, J. Matheson." Under the pressure of his finger, the rectangle lit up.

Greg shifted from foot to foot watching the keyterm. He talked randomly to Carmen, not really expecting an answer.

"It's been over a year since I was last here. Maybe a lot longer. What if my family isn't here anymore?" Greg pressed the Call Up button again. His green eyes passed over her without giving the impression of really seeing. "If only I could remember how it all started!" His tone held genuine frustration. "What excuse could've they been given for my absence?"

At long last, the screen flickered to life and a three-dimensional head and shoulders appeared."Who's there?" The woman's voice was pleasant enough, but it had a vaguely detached quality that reminded Carmen inexplicably of Donald after his Removal.

Greg stepped into view of the two-way screen. "It's me, Mom. Greg." To Carmen's utter astonishment his voice cracked a little. Carmen cocked her head to one side, puzzled. Was meeting one's Factor an important event? The Humanoids said not.

"No!" the little electronic face screamed. The word was stark with terror and it pulled Carmen's attention back to the screen. "No! You're a dream. Mr. Levensworth said so!" Hollows showed all too plainly in the woman's face.

Carmen was filled with a sudden uneasiness. She would not like to draw this face. It should not be put to paper.

The woman, Greg's Factor, made a move as if to break off communication and Greg threw himself into the breach. "Mother? Don't you know who I am? It's me, Greg. Don't shut me out," he pleaded.

The woman's hand went to her head as if it pained her. Tears ran down her face and she continued to repeat, "No! You're a dream."

"What do you mean?" Greg's was a cry from the heart. "I'm your son. Won't you please tell me what's going on?"

The woman's sobbing ceased and her chin lifted. "I do not have a son," she said coldly. "I never had a son. I just dream sometimes, that's all. There's no law against dreaming, is there?"

And then, as Greg opened his mouth to reply, her control broke and she practically screamed at him, "Why can't you just go away and leave me alone? If you were my real son, you would!" The picture cut off abruptly, the screen now a perfect blank.

"Hey!" Greg leaned furiously on the rectangle till it lit up again.

There was a small crackle before a businesslike voice came over the speaker. "This is Mrs. Matheson's nurse. Mrs. Matheson does not wish to talk to you. If you persist in ringing this bell, the security guard will be summoned."

"But I'm her son!" Greg protested in frustration. Then, when that got no response, he added desperately, "At least tell me where I can find my Dad or Lucy!"

There was a slight pause before the voice said, "I am not at liberty to divulge that information. Good day." There was a small click.

Greg pressed the button repeatedly, a look of blind panic settling over his face, but the peals were ignored. Carmen tugged at his arm and sighed with relief when he finally turned away. There was something about that voice. It reverberated down the corridors of her mind as if she had heard it before and under less-than-pleasant circumstances. She hurried Greg away as fast as she could. Carmen was unsure as to what exactly a security guard was, but she had little doubt that one had been called.

Greg's face had an oddly wooden look to it that Carmen didn't like. He didn't speak except to say, "So that's how they explained it. They wiped out my whole existence." She didn't need to ask who "they" were.

Carmen kept the silence between them until they had walked about twice the length of the Underground. "She must have cared about you a lot to Dream so much." When Greg still didn't reply, Carmen changed topic. "Who is Mr. Levensworth?"

"One of my teachers at school," he said sourly. "We weren't exactly on the best of terms. He was a real pain. One of the last things I remember was complaining about him to my friends. He'd just assigned a big report and given us two days to do it in! Can you imagine?" Greg's eyes flashed resentment.

Carmen, who was used to tighter deadlines, said nothing, leaning forward. She had never really wondered what caused Greg to be sent to the Underground in the first place.

"It was the standing joke in our group that he was inhuman," Greg said, finally opening up. "I even made a bet once with Rob about it." Greg smiled. "I had three days to prove Mr. Levensworth wasn't alive. I started with the most obvious thing: fingerprints. They're easy to pick up and everyone can't help but leave them around, right?" Greg was talking as he walked and didn't seem to expect answers. "Only somehow," he scowled, "I could never get any of his, not even smudges!"

The hairs on the back of Carmen's neck prickled as she looked at Greg uneasily. She didn't understand quite what a bet was, but had no doubt that it was a good way to ask for trouble.

"I tried a blood test next. A sample was harder to obtain, of course, but with a little ingenuity I managed it." The deviltry was back in Greg's eyes full force. "I was juggling three beakers during class and 'accidentally' hit Mr. Levensworth with one. It broke and cut his arm. Sure enough, he made me clean it up and it had a smear of blood on it. I tested it at home—" Greg paused for a deeper breath, "—it came out negative. Invalid data. It was late and I almost left it, but since I didn't feel the least bit sleepy, I redid it. It came out negative again. By now I was beginning to get a really weird feeling. No fingerprints and now this! I called up Rob and got him to come over. He touched it with his finger, tasted it and said, 'Very funny, Matheson. This is syrup.' And it was," Greg grinned. "Bright red syrup. Heaven knows how it got on my glass, but it did."

Carmen didn't think it was funny and she didn't ask him what *syrup* was. For once, she thought she knew. When she'd cut the two Humanoids up with her laser, they had leaked a sticky substance resembling blood. The awful feeling was back with her, as strong as it had been the first time. She clenched her hands into fists before asking, "What did you do then?"

Greg looked surprised. "Nothing. My three days were up. I paid Rob and a couple of days later my memory quits. The next thing I remember was waking up in the Underground." He looked into her eyes. "Why? You don't think Mr. Levensworth had anything to do with it, do you?"

"Yes, I do," Carmen said shortly. "He's a Humanoid." She remembered the ease of their escape with a suspicion bordering on fear. Even if she was wrong about Mr. Levensworth, it was obvious that Greg had forgotten something of importance between his paying Rob and his appearance in the Underground. The Humanoids had gone to extreme lengths to obtain Greg's silence. Why let him out now? *Unless he were no longer a threat at all!*

The urgency that Greg had talked about in escaping and alerting the Overworld hit Carmen. When Greg had said there were no Humanoids in the Overworld, time had seemed plentiful. Now, suddenly that luxury was lost to them.

"Come on!" Carmen grabbed Greg's arm. "We've got to hurry!"

Greg blinked. "Where are we going?"

Carmen stopped, perplexed; she really didn't know where. Who did one alert anyway? "To your—" she paused. How had Greg said it? *"—leader. Boss."*

"You mean the Grand Overseer." Greg looked around slowly. "City Works is this way," he gestured vaguely down the street they had just come up. Carmen started down it, walking fast, almost tempted to run. People did run in the Overworld, didn't they?

"Hang on!" Greg pulled back. He looked as if he were going to protest, but another look at Carmen's face changed his mind. He made a sharp left turn. "It'll be quicker if we just teleport."

"Teleport?" Carmen asked, though she did not slow down.

"It's a mode of travel. It'll take you wherever you want to go instantly, or at least to the nearest teleporting centre."

"How?" Carmen inquired.

A familiar grin spread over Greg's features. All he would say was "Wait and see."

The teleport was two blocks away to the south and she and Greg sped through both of them. There was a lineup in front of the platform and a machine that people were feeding pieces of paper. Carmen's curiosity got the better of her. "What are they putting in?"

"Money," Greg whispered back.

Worry struck her. Did they have any?

"Don't worry," Greg reassured her "We won't have to pay."

Carmen frowned. "But I thought you said—"

"Shh!" Greg now looked fully alert.

The person ahead stepped onto the platform and sat down. He pressed a button and, it seemed to Carmen, vanished into thin air. One minute the platform held a plump, bored man with his legs crossed; the next, nothing. She couldn't help but exclaim, "What happened to that man?"

Greg flashed a smile, two dimples appearing in his cheeks. "The same thing that's going to happen to us in a few minutes."

It was their turn in line. "Watch and learn." He pressed a small button labelled "Change" and scooped up the handful of round metal pieces that spilled out. He then reinserted them in another slot. "Nobody wants to carry around loonies anymore, so they don't pick up their change," he explained. The green light went on and they were allowed to proceed.

The platform itself had a number of dials and switches as well as a detailed map. Greg set their destination for Union.

"How long—" Carmen left her sentence dangling. There was a sudden vibration followed by a lurch. Carmen blinked. The buildings around them had vanished to be replaced with newer, even taller ones.

"Not long at all." Greg watched the look of surprise on her face with something like enjoyment. He put an arm around her waist and they stepped off the platform together. "This is the place." He went toward the widest and tallest of them all. It had no lock on its door and the sign proclaimed "City Works".

The inside looked almost bigger, if that were possible, and was filled with people, all moving purposefully about the business at hand.

Carmen, nudged Greg. "Which one is the Grand Overseer?"

Greg's lips twitched. "None of them," he whispered back. "The Overseer will be upstairs somewhere, Overseeing, no doubt. Follow me, and try not to look conspicuous." He started across the floor.

Carmen wasn't altogether sure she knew what he meant, but she was used to going unnoticed in a crowd of look-alike Children and her gliding walk was almost noiseless. Nobody stopped them or seemed to notice them in any way. They made it safely to an internal L-Vate. Before the sliding doors closed, Greg hurried her inside and pushed a button. "It's level fifteen if I remember correctly. They took us on a tour in Grade Nine."

The L-Vate lurched upward, startling her and causing an unpleasant sensation in her stomach. Greg grinned broadly. "Sure is an improvement over stairs, eh?"

Carmen smiled weakly. "Up to a point." She was glad to get out of the moving box and back into a bare-walled hallway. Except for the missing line down the centre, it wasn't all that much different from the Underground.

Aside from a single secretary huddled over an office keyterm, they reached the door reading "Grand Overseer" without meeting a soul. "Easy as pie," Greg said.

Besides being unsure of his metaphor, Carmen didn't like the sound of the "easy." But before she could pull back, the door slid open almost in their faces. Greg stepped in and she had no choice but to follow.

This room was also unadorned, dominated for the most part by a huge desk and chair in the centre of the room.

"Hello, Children," said the man in the chair. His voice had a familiar, musical ring to it, the memory of which Carmen would carry with her to the grave. It was the same politely human voice of Mrs. Matheson's nurse and, for that matter, of all the Humanoids. Only this one was all the more frightening because of the human face that went with it. "Carmen, Greg." He nodded politely to each in turn. "We've been expecting you."

CHAPTER TEN

Underground Again

Greg found his tongue first. "We are not Children!" His voice shook with anger.

"As you wish," the Humanoid said with equanimity. Steady blue eyes scrutinized them from out of a smooth, pinkish face. The face itself was perfectly human. Maybe a little too perfect. Not a hair on the Grand Overseer's head was out of place.

Greg masked his fear with a look of contempt. "We are here to see the Grand Overseer."

"I am the Grand Overseer," said the Humanoid. "How may I help you?"

Greg swore softly under his breath. He had guessed that the Humanoids must've had some contact high up, but the Grand Overseer himself? A third-rate chemohydrate teacher like Mr. Levensworth being one of them had been hard enough to believe, but to plant a stooge at this level called for more sophisticated capabilities—ones he hadn't credited the Humanoids with having.

"What are you going to do with us?" Carmen asked the question casually, her eyes on the cityscape out the window, but Greg noticed that her muscles were tensed and ready for a quick escape, if necessary.

"Why, nothing." The Overseer's human features expressed surprise. "We were going to bring you up here anyway."

Alarm bells jangled in Greg's head. They were contradicting themselves. Mr. Levensworth had been small potatoes compared to the Grand Overseer. Had they had shipped a snoopy Grade Thirteen student Underground rather than risk exposure on even that small a scale? "Aren't you afraid I might reveal the truth that you're not human and cause a panic?"

"You are of little importance. Your family already believes you nonexistent. Few people would even listen to your story." The Overseer ticked off the facts on its fingers.

"Then why bother taking me Underground at all? You could have just erased my memory and left me." Greg's frustration showed in his voice.

Surprisingly, it was Carmen who answered him. "There was an uneven number of Children that year." She turned her brilliant topaz eyes on the Grand Overseer. "That's why, isn't it?"

He nodded calmly. "Of course. Taking in Greg was a calculated risk from the beginning." He looked sadly towards Carmen. "We had not considered that he might contaminate one of our own Children."

Greg thought of Donald and Ilka and was doubly glad they had been left behind in the escape. Working from the inside they would eventually weaken the structure of the Underground, should Carmen and he fail. But he would not think of that possibility right now.

"That's it?" he said sarcastically, once the Overseer had remained silent. "We're free to go?"

"Yes." The Overseer had a way of answering questions that made them sound silly. "You may go."

But Greg wasn't willing to leave it at that. He had grown up wary of sudden reprieves. "I don't get it. What's the catch?" His voice was harsh. "How do you know we won't be believed?"

"We don't, of course," it answered coolly, "but what you say or do no longer matters. In twenty-one hours and fifty-seven minutes you will cease to be a problem. In fact, *all* your fellow humans on the face of the earth will cease to be a problem."

"How so?" Greg asked, a chill taking hold deep in his stomach. This was why escape had been so important. He remembered the Humanoid presentations with their orange skies and complete absence of human life.

For once, the Humanoid elaborated on its own. "Two hundred years ago when we were first created, you humans were bent on the extinction of your own kind. Our creators were peaceful, but their Government wanted to use us as a weapon even though you already had the nuclear capability to blow up the world many times over."

Hot words of denial rose to Greg's lips, but then he remembered an oblique reference to the Nuclear Age in one of his textbooks. Humankind had been overconfident and foolish at the time. It was possible.

"Of course," the Humanoid went on, "it was not in our best interests to let this happen. As it became more and more obvious that humans were unfit to govern themselves, we stepped quietly in. We had no choice. Too often their decisions were based on mistrust and emotion. We began to implement a socio-political system based on logic and psychocybernetic efficiency. Naturally, a transfer of power was in order, but you *humans*," it said the word with pronounced condescension, "were, as always, prone to panic at any hint of a loss of your precious free will, so these benevolent disguises—" it pulled at the phony flesh on its arm, "—became necessary."

Greg clenched his fists. "Those humans," he said bitingly, "happened to be the ones who created you, you worthless pile of junk!"

His intended insult was ignored. "But their brilliance in certain areas was overshadowed by their superstitious fears and morbid concern with outward appearances. Our peaceful Creators were no exception. Even they had to be contained when they learned how we planned to save the planet from perishing." The Grand Overseer shook its head sadly. "Self-governed human beings never learn. They are illogical to the last."

"You're the one that's illogical!" Greg burst out. "Why save us once, only to wipe out the whole human race now?"

"We have no intention of *discontinuing* the human race." The Grand Overseer shook its head slowly. "Just the opposite. We have great hopes of maintaining a model human civilization. Why do you think we went to all the expense of setting up Underground systems across the face of the earth? When it became obvious that, despite all our help, the Overworld was doomed, we had to devise a plan for salvation using the material at hand.

"It was first necessary to break the cycle of contamination. We removed selected Children from the influence of their Factors and began to reshape human destiny." The Humanoid's eyes glowed cobalt blue. "We set up a process of re-education. If, by using psychosurgery, we can replace emotion with logic, the human being will become an incredible thinking tool. Especially when you consider at present a human utilizes only a minor percentage of the brain. A human can do things we cannot: you can generate new ideas."

The cobalt eyes turned on Carmen. "Human creativity is a precious gift and must not be wasted on things of lesser quality. Your Drawings were of lesser quality. With our help, the good which humans do will be separated from the bad and the world will become perfect."

Carmen's face burned with humiliation, but she said nothing.

"We are now entering the next phase of our Plan," the Grand Overseer continued. "The Children have progressed as far as it is possible Underground. The new challenges and opportunities of the Overworld are necessary for their successful adaptation. The humans presently covering the face of the earth are now obsolete and they therefore must make way. And, since neither of you no longer meet our psychometric standards of mental purity, you will be terminated." It spoke calmly, as if the deed had already been done. "Nothing must stand in the way of the Children."

"The road to hell," Greg said suddenly, "is paved with good intentions."

The Grand Overseer's eyebrows pulled together in a human frown, but its puzzlement lasted only a few seconds. "A popular human proverb, I believe, attributable to a combination of St. Bernard and Samuel Johnson.

Entirely inapplicable, of course." It passed on without pause. "I said, you are free to go now." And, as an afterthought, it added, "Re-entry into the Underground is, of course, prohibited."

Greg was about to say, "Fine with me. You couldn't make me go back," when it hit him that he wasn't alone in this mess. He had dragged Carmen into it as well. Guilt flayed him. If it weren't for him, she at least would be safe, a protected Child. "Not even Carmen?" asked Greg, beginning to talk quickly. "She's one of the Children. You can't just leave her here to die! Just erase her memory like you did before." He pleaded even though he knew it was useless. "I'm the troublemaker! Don't Punish Carmen!"

The unyielding face of the Overseer told the story even before it spoke. "No. It has been proven that her brain is contaminated beyond our capacity to cleanse it."

Greg's face crumpled. For the first time since Grade Three, he felt like crying. Carmen moved over beside him, resting her hand lightly on his shoulders. "I would not go back down there without you."

Greg straightened. Now was not the time for recriminations. They weren't dead yet. He looked around with an air of determination.

The Humanoid began to punch up codes on its computer. "You may go now."

Grasping at its words, Greg intended to be stubborn. "But we don't have to, do we? I mean, after all, we're not important," he said silkily.

The Humanoid blinked, but it fell into the trap without hesitation. "It does not matter what you do. If you try to alter the course of destiny as we have defined it, you will, of course, be terminated. Do not think you will escape as easily as last time. We have lasers, too."

A plan was beginning to form in Greg's head. "Good." He could feel Carmen's questioning eyes on him. Steering her off to one side, Greg began talking to Carmen in a whisper. "I'm not giving up. They may think we're *personae non gratae*, but that's all to the better. If we're not important, they won't hesitate to answer questions, right?"

Carmen nodded affirmative, the spark of hope growing in her eyes.

"The way I see it, we already have one advantage over these tin cans."

"What's that?"

Greg grinned wickedly. "They don't know how to lie. They may slant the truth horribly and tell only half of it, but it's still the truth. They haven't the imagination for even one really good lie. You heard what the robot said. Creatively a newborn baby is far superior to them. We'll have to play it by ear for a while. "

With a wink at Carmen, Greg turned back to the Grand Overseer and started in right away. No sense giving the Humanoid a moment to order them out.

"How are you going to annihilate us all without killing yourselves as well?" asked Greg.

The Humanoid had no qualms about answering. "By taking advantage of ingenious human technology. Before the end of the so-called Nuclear Age, a bomb was developed strictly for human termination. This Neutron Bomb, as they called it, was designed to wipe an area clean of its inhabitants, but leave the real estate intact. Buildings, vehicles, and important things like records and scientific data would be left undisturbed, ready for the next set of tenants." A cold, smug smile spread across the face of the Grand Overseer. "To be expected, there are a few adverse side effects to meganeutronic saturation, but we estimate that even the orange sky will fade in a little more than a hundred years. In the meantime, the Children will just have to take their radioactivites."

Greg had to stop and swallow the ugly words that rose inside of him. Carmen stepped in smoothly. "How many bombs? What kind of range do they have?"

"How thoughtful of you to ask! Suffice it to say that, thanks to human ingenuity, no corner of the earth's surface will escape unscathed. Every centre of population has generously been provided with a Neutron Bomb capable of servicing its constituent residency."

"How are they activated?" asked Carmen. "Is it done separately or all at once?"

The Overseer shifted uneasily. It must have sensed some kind of trap, because it hesitated for a second, whirring, as if rechecking permission to tell. The response must have come back affirmative for it did answer. "It will happen at the same time, at Central's command, but each must be accessed separately.

"Where's Central?"

"In Ellay." Greg's heart sank. It had named a city on the opposite coast, thousands of kilometres distant. "Entry there is also prohibited." Greg turned a defeated look towards Carmen. What now? he telegraphed silently.

The old steadiness and concentration showed in Carmen's face. She hadn't given up. But her question did not make much sense to him. "Do all Programmers use the latest AlphaBeta 1.1 release?"

It took the Humanoid a moment to adjust. "Yes."

"Can this keyterm access the Programming shell?"

It smiled. "For security reasons, no."

Her next questions made even less sense and Greg almost thought she must be trying to confuse the robot, but the directness of her eyes made him unsure. Carmen was basically unused to deception and he wasn't sure she was that much of an actress. She fired them off, one after another: "Which Creator programmed you?" and "Where were you programmed?" and "What SysAdmin Level are you at?"

Following each answer she would nod as if fixing the data in her head. And, finally, after she had discovered which networking protocols were shared among the Undergrounds, she made a beeline for the door. Greg wasn't far behind her. "What was that all about?"

Carmen gave him a Humanoidal look that spelled out ISN'T IT OBVIOUS? in capital letters. "We just have to Reprogram them."

"To correct the mistakes of the Creators?"

"If I have enough time," said Carmen.

Greg looked at his wrist out of habit, but his watch was long gone. That had been one of the things that had puzzled Carmen. Why did the mention of time make him look at his wrist? Overworlders were so complex!

"Wouldn't that mean returning to the Underground to find a Humanoid keyterm?" Greg didn't looked thrilled at the prospect.

"Yes."

He was going to point out that re-entry was prohibited, but since when had a little thing like that ever stopped Greg Matheson? Somehow returning to the Underground would be like going back to prison. Which was silly because the Underground alone would be safe when the bombs went off. *If* the bombs went off, Greg corrected himself. They wouldn't, if he had anything to say about it.

Carmen was talking and Greg hastily refocussed his attention on what she was saying. "They will have put some kind of guard up at the old subway station where we surfaced," she reasoned. "We need to find an alternate entrance."

Greg nodded. It was their only shot. "We had better take the teleport." There was little time for scenic routes today.

The line at Union Station seemed miles long. When the man in front of them checked the change compartment, Greg felt like screaming, "No, you can't! That's ours. We need it more!" Luckily, the man only withdrew a loonie. There was more than enough left to teleport him and Carmen down to within a block of the old subway entrance.

Acting on the slim chance that the Humanoids had been lying or didn't have a chance to block off the tunnel, Greg ran down the street only to halt in horror. The entrance they had come out of had not just been locked; the entire subway tunnel had been collapsed over top of it. The Humanoids must have dynoploded it. A team of bulldozers would be needed to get in now. Even then, finding the door would be like looking for a neutrino in an A-stack.

Carmen did not share his disappointment; she had expected it. "Humanoids never bluff."

They did the only thing they could do; they started searching for another way in. They separated and yelled out possible ideas to each other. Some areas they searched three times while others were only glanced over. Greg racked his brain for all the logical places. They had nothing to eat and it seemed they had been there looking forever. But every time Greg found himself lagging, the thought would cross his mind of how few hours the world had left and he would redouble his efforts. He knew the same thought spurred on Carmen. The absence of a digitime—or even a watch—only heightened the effect.

Carmen noticed the gradual setting of the sun and coming of night first. She searched even harder, but in the end the darkness beat her. Greg called for a stop. They weren't doing any good as it was: they were both bone-tired and, while the city never got fully dark, it was not the safest place to be out in.

It had also cooled down considerably and Carmen, who had never experienced anything but a regulated temperature, was soon shivering. Greg wondered if the Humanoids had thought to take that into the Children's preparation. He located a small, sheltered gap between two buildings and headed for it, but Carmen hung back.

It took him a moment to figure out why. When he did he wanted to laugh—and hold her. Carmen, for whom he had had to define the word *fear* and who had stood up to the Humanoids on numerous occasions, was afraid of the dark. He had never seen anyone as rational as Carmen act so irrationally.

"It's only night coming on."

"*Night?* Like we learned about in the holoshow?" Carmen waved at the darkening sky.

"Yes."

"What if it's an unscheduled failure of the Sun's power source."

"It's not."

"Are you sure?"

"Come here," said Greg and took her hand.

He found a place where the ground was not rock-hard and hollowed out a place to sit, leaning against the wall. They watched the sun go down in a blaze of orange and it took much convincing on Greg's part for Carmen to believe they weren't already too late and that the end of the Overworld had come. She cuddled up to him. "For warmth!" And Greg tried his best to distract her—with jokes, put-downs of the Humanoids, and a few hoary stories of the Overworld. Fatigue hit and they were both asleep within the hour.

Greg awoke in a mild panic. He crawled to the entrance way and looked out at the city to find it buzzing and the skies alight with sunshine. His mind raced frantically, trying to remember directions and figure the approximate position of the sun. He shaded his eyes, it was quite bright now. How long had the sun been up? *How many hours had they wasted?*

"Carmen!" he yelled loudly, not moving from his position by the street. "We've got to get going." He was about to shout "hurry," but Carmen appeared, swift and silent as a shadow at his side. She saw the sun and guessed the reason behind his anxiety.

Her face was white and her voice quiet when she said, "At most, we have seven hours left." The least was not a topic they discussed.

Greg's stomach growled, reminding him of more immediate worries. He was starving and Carmen probably was, too. "We're not going to get anything done if we don't eat. I'm going to round something up. You stay here."

"How about I meet you at the site?" she asked, clipping on her laser.

"Sounds okay to me. See you soon." Greg jogged back out onto the street. The L-Vate ships were gone, leaving this part of the city almost deserted. His hunger now a gnawing pain, he kept jogging until he was among people. Green eyes sharp, Greg slowed down, watching the people around him. Without money, his options were limited to stealing or rummaging through garbage cans. Neither choice much appealed to him.

A fat man passed him, munching on a chocobar and carrying a package of five others. Greg abruptly reversed, following the man. He'd had more than enough of nutrition when he was in the Underground.

Greg was just about to grab the chocobars and run when the fat man suddenly stopped. His round mouth *Ohhed*! in horror and his eyes bulged as a red-haired woman bore down on him. "Mandy!" he smiled nervously, trying to conceal the package behind his back. "What a nice surprise!"

Mandy didn't smile back. She pounced unerringly on the chocobars. "Have you forgotten your diet already? For shame!" She tossed the chocobars at a litterslot, but Greg intercepted them in midair. As Greg jogged off, the fat man followed his chocobars with mournful eyes.

Chocobars! Greg couldn't believe his luck. Carmen was in for a real treat—her first meal in the Overworld.

Carmen was not so sure. She studied the plastic-wrapped brown bars with misgiving. "This is your Food? It's brown."

"Just try it." Greg's eyes danced. He unwrapped a chocobar of his own and took a bite. "M'good," he mumbled through a full mouth.

Carmen sniffed at her chocobar before cautiously taking a nibble. An expression of astonishment crossed her face, and Greg laughed. "Well, what do you think?"

"It tastes funny. Kind of like $C_{12}H_{22}O_{11}$." Carmen named the chemical formula for sugar.

"It should. That's one of the major ingredients." Greg took another huge bite and Carmen followed suit. When the last of the chocobars was gone Carmen licked her fingers and sighed, "I can see why you prefer it to Food."

Then, without a word, they turned and resumed the search, going farther afield and double-checking. At first it was almost pleasant under the warm morning sun, but as each possibility turned to dust, a kind of desperation settled over the junk-strewn field. Fear kept pace at Greg's side like some fiendish companion; thought of eating or resting never crossed his mind. At least not for long.

Carmen called for help in moving a big rock and, after sweating and pushing a lot, they managed to roll it to one side. There was no concealed door under it. Greg sat down for a moment, breathing hard. "This could scarcely be more work," he observed, "than if we were digging into the Underground." His face took on an arrested expression. "Carmen," he said, an undercurrent of excitement in his voice, "What material was the roof of the Underground made of? Do you remember?"

Carmen caught on at once, an electric smile lighting her face. "Concrete! I remember thinking it must be really old to have been built of that flimsy material."

The half-hidden ground to the left of the buried subway seemed the logical place to start. Greg collected a few outdated hand tools, including something he called a *shovel*, from the old subway. As a plan, it was hardly flawless. Greg had no real idea where to dig, so they chose a low spot they both agreed would be the most likely. After the third shovelful, Greg changed his mind about the ease of the work. Carmen volunteered to trade off with him a few times, but the shovel was really too big and awkward for her to handle. Greg did most of the digging while she hauled the dirt away in an old oil bucket.

Greg dug until he had blisters and aching back muscles. And then he dug some more. There were times he felt like giving up and laying down, but the sight of Carmen prodded him on. With sweat on her brow and eyes that wouldn't give up, her face was a picture of determination. Greg turned back to his task and kept on.

Then, finally, after what seemed like hours, his shovel hit something solid. The metallic clank was the sweetest sound he could imagine. Quickly, he cleared away the dirt to reveal a broad expanse of concrete. There was no guarantee that this was the Underground's roof, but Greg's heart lightened tremendously when he saw it. What fools the old builders must have been to construct it of this, and how he thanked them for it now! Concrete could be sliced with a laser, unlike the nuke-proof Durabuilt used in today's buildings.

"Laser, please." Greg held out his hand. Carmen unclipped it and gave it to him. He aimed it at the edge of the hole he'd dug and cut roughly around its perimeter. He took care to maintain an angle which would allow the concrete to fall into the room below—if there were a room below. The burning concrete threw off a gray smoke which smelled like the essence of dryness. Greg grinned as he came close to completing the circle, but then the laser started to splutter.

"I wondered how long the battery would last," said Carmen. "Lasers draw a tremendous amount of energy."

"Well, so much for technology," said Greg, tossing aside the spent laser. "I guess we'll just have to break through using fleshopounds." Keeping one foot on the outside of the laser-cut line, he stamped with his other on the concrete inside the line. Nothing happened. He stamped harder. When the concrete plug remained intact, Greg lost his temper and jumped right in the middle with both feet.

"Don't!" Carmen cried, leaping forward. Too late! There was a great cracking sound as Greg and the concrete plug disappeared from view. Only his instinctive grab for the edge saved Greg from crashing down with it. He hung there dangling until Carmen could position herself to help haul him up. As he lay panting beside her, Greg noticed her face was whiter than usual and there might even have been tears shining in her eyes.

"Carmen, why did you shoot the Humanoids?"

Carmen froze. "I, I don't know," she said at long last, but for the first time Greg was aware that she was not being completely up front with him.

A faint hope fanned itself to combustion within him. "It wouldn't be because—because you remember me?" He held his breath.

Carmen wasted no time in dashing that thought to pieces. "No!"

When he winced, her voice softened and reached out. "Greg?" He sat up to look at her. She picked her words carefully, weighing each one as she went along. "It is true that I don't remember you, but—" she hesitated, then went bravely on, "—if you were to Ask, I would be your Chosen."

Greg wasted no time. "Carmen, will you be my Chosen?"

Carmen blinked. "I just said I would."

A laugh bubbled up in Greg's throat. "You're supposed to say yes."

"Yes," Carmen said obediently. Smiling, he kissed her on the nose and she looked up at him curiously. "What was that for?"

"Never mind." Greg could feel his face and ears turning red again. He turned towards the rough-hewn hole to hide his embarrassment. "Come on," he said, almost brusquely. "We're wasting time. I'll lower you down first and then myself."

The concrete plug made the distance to the floor shorter. With the added length of Greg's arms, Carmen was able to make the drop quite safely. She moved out of the way and signalled for him to come down.

Hanging from the edge, he dropped lightly, landing in a crouched position. The clean-cut concrete had torn at his hands, drawing blood. "Ouch!" he exhaled. "That—" His words broke off suddenly as his eyes took in what appeared to be an empty room. Carmen wasn't there!

Greg bit his lip. What was happening? Where was Carmen? Memories of the morning after her Removal came rushing back to him with sickening clarity. Had the Humanoids gotten her again? And here he was without a weapon!

Heart hammering, Greg approached the door. He dared not call Carmen's name in case there were Ears around. He poked his head around the doorway just in time to see a flash of metal go round the next corner. And with the metal a bit of white—white like Carmen's jumpsuit.

Greg didn't stop to calculate odds, but just charged down the hallway in hot pursuit. There she was, being dragged away by a Humanoid guard! Carmen saw Greg before the guard did, so she dived quickly to one side leaving the Humanoid open for attack. Greg had never been the smallest or shyest of the Tronno B.J.'s and generally, when he pushed something, it moved. The Humanoid was no exception; one good old-fashioned body check and it was down and out of the game.

Greg removed his shoe in a flash and was ready to strike, if necessary, but the Humanoid didn't move. Its blue lights first dimmed, flickered once, and then fizzled completely. Greg smiled grimly. Apparently the Humanoid's delicate circuitry wasn't designed for a little Noram I-Tag action.

"You've killed it!" Carmen sounded awed.

Greg glanced up. "You can't kill something that was never alive." He flicked the silver plating on the Humanoid contemptuously. "It's repairable."

Carmen shivered. "We had better hurry. This seems to be the only Humanoid up on this level, but if it already reported on the noise and fails to make contact within the next quarter hour, they will come checking."

Greg nodded. That gave them less than fifteen minutes. They had to start Reprogramming. Now. He looked around in exasperation. "We have to find the Programmer."

"We really only need a keyterm," corrected Carmen. When Greg looked at her quizzically, she continued. "The Humanoid was taking me this way. Presumably its office is down this hall." Carmen and Greg exchanged glances, and of one accord began to run.

They came to a cramped little room just off the main hallway. Inside, on a built-in desk, sat a miliforce-issue keyterm, its screen glowing a pale, pale blue. A cursor blinked steadily on the command line: the guard hadn't had time to log out.

"Can you run it?" Greg asked.

She looked uneasy. "Maybe. But first we have to clear this up."

One tiny line on the computer screen made Greg's blood chill: INVEST PRESSURE DROP UPPER SECTOR. REPORT IMMED.

"We must have thrown off the air pressure when we broke in," said Carmen. "Command Central is asking for an explanation."

"What will we do?" He knew that one wrong stroke on the keyboard could give the game away.

Carmen's long silence did not bode well with Greg. He was careful to keep out of the way while she sat down in front of the glowing tube and studied it.

When the computer flashed on another line, it startled them both. REPORT DUE NOW, blinked ominously on the screen.

Carmen started to type: FAULTY SENSOR UPPER SECTOR.

"That ought to hold them for a while," said Carmen. "But we really need to get out of this shell level and up to where we can do something." She typed: REQUEST PERM SYSADMIN LEVEL 3.

The answer was immediate: PERM DENIED.

"Well, we are not going to get into System Administration by being polite," said Carmen. "Let me try something else." She pounded in a series of commands which, to Greg, looked like ancient Californspeak. The screen all of a sudden went blank. When Carmen carefully tapped in one keystroke after another, nothing showed. "Let's hope my old backdoor works."

The screen responded: SYSADMIN LEVEL 3 AND WAITING.

For the first time, Carmen looked up and smiled. "Lucky I put in that old password shortcut back when I was in SysAdmin Project."

KILL INVEST PRESSURE DROP UPPER SECTOR, she typed, saying, "So much for their concern over our break in."

"Now that we're in and clear, can you do it?" asked Greg nervously.

"That was the easy part. Now I have to find my way to the main Programmer in Ellay. I never knew other Undergrounds existed till today." She turned to Greg; her topaz eyes seemed to bore right through him. "I have to really concentrate now." He had never seen her quite like this before. In control.

He kept very quiet as the screen filled up with strange symbols. The room was silent save for the click of the keys and the squeak of the wheels on her chair. Greg sat on the floor and leaned on the wall opposite, but he found himself bursting with worry. On top of that, his stomach was growling. How long would it take to do a complete Reprogramming and run it? And how much of that time did they have? An hour, two hours, twenty-five minutes?

He found himself at Carmen's shoulder again, trying not to hover but not managing very well. He would have felt a lot more comfortable at the keyterm himself punching in codes, but with only a limited Overworld school training he couldn't hope to program anything. In the sciences, the Children were by far his superiors. The Humanoids had succeeded in that respect.

Greg watched for as long as he could bear—it seemed to take an eternity although Carmen's fingers were literally a blur over the keys—and then he went for a short walk around the hallways. Within minutes he was back. He had a headache by now, far worse than any previous one he had ever had, and the worry kept growing. The not knowing was the worst. Carmen had estimated seven hours that morning and a good five or six had been gobbled up since then. What if she had overestimated? What if it was already too late?

He could keep still no longer. Greg was about to tell Carmen he was going to scout around a bit, then thought better of it. In the doorway, he took one look back to see her long fingers flying over the keyboard. As he made his way back to where they had broken in, he reminded himself that muscle was his department.

He found a piece of rebar sticking out of the concrete plug large enough for a good billy stick, so he set to working it back and forth until it snapped off.

"Now I'm ready for anything." He tapped the metal bar onto the palm of his left hand and headed back to explore the hallways past the guard's office. As he passed the doorway, he heard Carmen talking to herself in some strange tongue.

It didn't take long to case out the Upper Sector. Greg located the staircase that must descend to the Underground proper. Holding his breath, he listened down its long corridor for any sound of activity. None, there was none. But then, he heard a faint but steady thump, thump, thump. "Get ahold of yourself, Matheson," he instructed himself. "That's just your own heartbeat." He listened some more just to be sure before returning to Carmen at the keyboard.

"I'm running into some flak in Ellay," she said, looking worried. "The access codes to the Neutron Bombs are waxed over."

"Can't you just shut off their power?"

"Nice try, but they put in a dedicated power source back in the late twentieth century. No, I have to get in there and deactivate the timers myself." Then she was off again, in her own world of hexcodes and compilers, muttering words Greg had never dreamt of. It all became a bit of a blur for him: he was all keyed up and had nothing to do. He was brought to suddenly, when she let out a swear word and hit the desktop with her fist. He *had* been a bad influence on her.

"I better check the staircase again." Greg ducked out of the room and hiked down the hall.

Greg listened again at the doorway down. His heart just about stopped. He distinctly heard footsteps this time, and more than one set, scraping on the grit of the staircase. Humanoids! He eased the large metal door shut as quietly as he could. If he could only jam it somehow. Greg ran back to the lifeless body of the guard and dragged it to the entrance to the stairway. He stuffed it in front of the door as best he could. Then he ran at top speed back to Carmen.

"Humanoids!" he gasped. "Coming up the steps. Can you cut the power in the Underground?"

Even before he finished asking, she shook her head. "If I cut the power, my keyterm goes too. You'll—" The machine beeped peevishly and Carmen went back to her keyboard. Her voice trailed after him down the hallway. "I'm into Ellay."

Greg turned the last corner before the stairway entrance and stopped dead. Two Humanoids were bending over the fallen body of the guard. They were carrying some type of hand weapon he had never seen before.

"Possibility," one Humanoid said, "the motor-area board could have failed."

"But the Ears have picked up organic activity in Upper Sector," said the other. "Let us separate and meet in the guard's office."

Hiding behind the corner, Greg tightened his grip on the rebar. As the footsteps drew nearer, he found he couldn't swallow. There was an enormous lump in his throat and he felt his body stiffen up, just like in International Tag, only the stakes were a lot higher here. What if he couldn't move when the time came?

He needn't have worried. When the Humanoid rounded the corner, Greg wrapped the rebar around its face. Without so much as a bleep, it sunk to its knees and toppled forward. Its gun clattered to the floor.

Greg dropped the rebar and scooped up the gun. The guardroom! The Humanoid would be heading there next.

He returned just in time to hear telltale metallic footsteps approaching from down the nearest corridor.

Greg levelled the gun chest-high towards the far corner and waited. When the Humanoid rounded the corner, he squeezed the trigger.

Ptang! A projectile ricocheted off the Humanoid's breastplate and came skittering back down the hall to stop at Greg's feet. It was a tiny tranquilizer dart, its bent needle oozing pink liquid. The Humanoid slowly raised its gun at Greg. "We will not hurt you," it soothed and began walking towards him. "We will not hurt you."

Greg dashed into the guard's office. "Carmen, get off that chair!" he screamed, almost out of control. "I need it!

She stood up and pushed the chair over to him. Her face was calm with an unearthly glow. Her eyes locked onto Greg's as she spoke. "I love you."

It was a reborn Greg who leaped out the door holding the chair before him as a shield.

"We will not hurt you," went the Humanoid. *Pfft!* went the dart gun. *Kthuk!* went the dart into the bottom of the chair.

Ksmash! went the chair as it shattered into pieces over the Humanoid's motor area.

Greg's victory was short-lived. Within twelve seconds, a great scuffling of footsteps came down the hall from towards the staircase. He heard orders being given and Humanoids spreading out down all the hallways.

Greg ran back into the guard's office and, as gently as he could, put his hands on Carmen's shoulders. She was half-sitting, half-kneeling on her heel. "Carmen ..." he gasped, trying to catch his breath.

"Just give me a minute," she said vaguely. "The Reprogramming is almost done."

"Forget the Reprogramming!" shouted Greg. "Shut everything down or we're dead!" He watched as Carmen switched commands silently. She stared at the computer console as if it were a thing alive, concentrating.

"I'll tack on a local domestic shutdown," she said calmly at long last. "Just hold them off one more minute."

Just another minute! Knowing she had her job to do and he had his should have provided Greg with some relief, but it didn't. Instead, the tension behind his eyes increased. All he could do was pace around the room, shaking his fists.

"There." The small word from her lips was explosive in the room. Greg turned back from his countless circuits around the floor. Carmen pressed the return button and there was a pause.

ARE YOU SURE? asked the keyterm.

She typed Y and covered her face with shaking hands, slumping down against the wall. She had done all she could.

The screen at first held steady. Then, one by one, lines began to flash, one beneath the other.

NYORK DEACTED.

LUNNON DEACTED.

VANCOV DEACTED.

MOSC DEACTED.

ELLAY DEACTED.

EDMTON DEACTED.

The list went on and on until it was a ripply blue stream, jiggling and flowing up the screen.

Carmen threw herself into Greg's arms. "There wasn't time to do them in alphabetical order!" She broke into huge, heaving sobs. Her face, hot and sticky with tears, burrowed into his neck.

"There, there," was all Greg could say. "There, there." He thought he was beginning to sound like a psychosoothing Humanoid. He kept his wits about him and his eye on the door. "There, there."

"I hate this," Carmen said on a ragged note. "The waiting and wondering. It's all up to the main computer in Ellay now, and it may still be too late. Don't ask me why, but because we're here, Tronno has to be deacted last." She snuffled once and seemed to pull herself together. "I guess it has something to do with keeping the line open to the keyterm in command."

The hair prickled up on the back of Greg's neck. Weren't they out of the woods yet?! "Shhh. It's okay, Carmen," he whispered into her ear. "It's going to be all right." Words of comfort were meaningless and they both knew it, but, as the metallic footsteps drew nearer and nearer, they were all Greg had to offer.

Neatly framed in the doorway stood two Humanoids, dartguns at the ready. "We will not hurt you," they psychosoothed in unison. The stream on the screen abruptly halted. Something was happening, either sky-high nuclear holocaust or the shutdown. Greg held his breath.

The lights went out.

C H A P T E R   E L E V E N

Freedom

In the darkness, Carmen froze. Neither she nor Greg even breathed, and when the Humanoids crashed powerless to the floor, it was somehow irrelevant. They were both listening, straining their ears for the sound of an explosion that never came.

Carmen let her breath out in stages. "We did it. We actually did it." Her voice was a thin, thready sound.

"*We* did it? *You* did it!" Greg bent down until their foreheads touched. "Congratulations, Miss World-Saver!" He gave her a kiss, only in the dark he missed and it landed nearer her ear than her mouth.

Carmen laughed; she couldn't help it, and Greg joined in. It felt good to laugh, something they hadn't done for a long, long time. When at last they stopped, they lapsed into silence again. Comfortable silence.

Sounds began to reach up to them from the levels below, screaming and crying mixed in with the odd crash. Carmen felt Greg tense up. "I suppose we'd better start sorting things out," he said. "Who's directly below us?"

"The Factors Squared, I think. That or the Factors themselves." Carmen wasn't exactly sure.

"Well," said Greg, "whoever they are, they're first on our list. Here, hold my hand. We'll have to make our way down the staircase." She held firmly onto Greg's hand and let him lead the way, reflecting that there was a certain advantage to being scared of the dark.

Every once in a while they had to step over the bodies of deactivated Humanoids. Brushing her foot or an ankle against their cold metal plating made her shiver.

Greg found the door to the staircase with little difficulty. The steps, she discovered, were harder to negotiate in the dark. Carmen was glad more than once for the support Greg offered her.

It wasn't difficult to find the door to the first level: it had a landing on it. When Greg pulled the door open, human noises spilled out over them. A mixture of voices were all talking at once. Someone was sobbing in the background. Greg pulled Carmen closer to him and said, "Cover your ears." He took a deep breath and yelled hello as loud as he could.

Instant silence! Then one crusty, old voice spoke up. "There's no need to shout. We aren't all deaf yet."

"Sorry," Greg said in a more normal tone, "I just wanted to get your attention."

"Well, you've got it," the voice remarked dryly. "Supposing you tell us what's going on here?" There was a babble of agreement from the others.

Carmen replied this time. "We turned off the power. The Humanoids are no more."

There were several gasps and one "Alleluia," but Carmen noticed that none of them came from the old man. Carmen could hear him taking laboured steps forward. When he found Greg and Carmen, he took their hands and held them tightly. "You must be part of the Noram Miliforce to have knocked out the Humanoids."

"No," laughed Greg. "There are only two of us. How many of you?"

The old man chuckled. It was a wheezy sound, oddly magnified in the dark. "There are fifteen of us in all. Why are you here? To rescue us?" he sounded almost sarcastic.

"Well, yes. Actually we are," Greg began. "We—"

Carmen cut him off. Her curiosity was getting the best of her again. "Who are you?"

"Me, or us in general?" The old man didn't wait for an answer. "My name is David and officially we are the Factors Squared. We were among the first to get in on the Great Experiment—the one where those miserable robots took our children from us and dared to call it a Kindness." David's voice held bitter outrage. "Half of us were born here like me, and the other half in the Overworld. Like Jenny," he sighed. "Poor Jenny always did say we'd escape some day."

"Jenny?" Carmen asked quickly. Greg tugged as her hand impatiently, but she ignored him. "My Factors are J, D, C and R."

There was another moment of absolute silence. "Well, I'll be a— What's your name, girl?"

"Carmen."

After that, it was pure chaos as all the Factors Squared jumped into the conversation. Did she know of any Children with the Factors L and T? Were there any girls named Eleanor?

They crowded in on her until Greg eventually had to put a stop to it by yelling for quiet. "Look," he said, "I know you're all very eager to find out about your grandchildren, but, believe me, now is not the time. We came here first because you are closest to the top. There are other Groups that need to be rescued as well."

There was an immediate upsurge of voices volunteering to help with the rescue operation. With David's help, several parties of two or more each were formed. One was in charge of the evacuation and guiding the people through the dark up to where Greg and Carmen had come through. The search was on.

The next level down were the Factors, where there was again much crying and laughing while families were reunited and lost members mourned. Carmen and Greg left them, their feet clattering down the steps in the dark.

They passed by a long stretch with no doors. This was the place that Carmen remembered as making a soft humming noise when they had dashed by it before. It had probably housed all the machinery that kept the Underground running. Silence reigned now.

In fact, the unnatural quiet continued down onto the next level—the Children's level. Carmen's fingers were shaking as she helped Greg slide the door open. The first room, Carmen's Empty Room, was deserted, of course, as was the Forbidden Hallway. And the Exercise Room. It wasn't until they approached the Assembly did they hear any murmur of noise.

Suddenly fearful, Carmen stopped outside the door, preventing Greg from going in. "Shh!" she cautioned. Someone was talking about the Overworld. Carmen's heart warmed when she recognized the voice of the speaker. "It's Donald!" she said under her breath.

"So, why are you whispering?" Carmen had no reply to that, so Greg pushed open the door and called, "Hey, Donald!" It wasn't quite as loud as his first hello, but Carmen still winced.

"Greg?" Donald answered back, in tones of incredulity. "Is that you?"

"And me," Carmen piped up.

The crowd was on them in a flash. Here for the first time was light, taken from several of the Projects. Smiling faces were everywhere. It seemed each of the Children had to touch Greg and Carmen before they believed their good fortune.

"I knew it! I knew it!" Donald exclaimed gleefully. "When the lights went out, I knew it had to be you guys."

"Well, you were right," Greg confirmed. "Is everyone here?"

"Not exactly." Donald looked grim. "We found Belle down on the floor. Dead. She was one of the Humanoids. When the lights went out, she fell with them."

Carmen made a small exclamation. Things were beginning to fall into place. She had wondered how the Humanoids had known that Greg was spreading around talk of the Overworld.

Donald looked at her curiously, but as she kept her thoughts to herself, he went on. "Then all *hell* broke loose." He glanced at Greg. "We were just starting to get organized when you came in. We took a vote and everyone was in favour of escaping to the Overworld. We were just planning how best to rescue the Factors and Factors Squared when you came in." Donald beamed at them both.

"No problem," Greg said smoothly. "Just follow me." Between Carmen and Greg and Donald, they managed to herd everybody into the Empty Room and up the stairs. David's group would help show them the rest of the way.

Carmen had just put her foot on the first step when the sound of muffled wailing reached them from below. She started, memory flooding back. "Oh! I forgot. There's another level down below us. We've got to get going."

"Need some help?" Ilka asked. Donald was right there, too.

"I don't know what I'd do without you two," Carmen said warmly. Donald led the way with a laser light. The four of them descended further into the Underground, one step at a time.

They had gone no further than fifty or sixty steps when the noise hit them—real crying here with top-of-the-lung screaming. Carmen passed Donald in her hurry downward, heedless of the deepening shadows. She had been in Medical Project: she could help.

Greg was right behind her and helped to slide the door open. Carmen rushed right in, following the sound of crying, and nearly tripped over a Humanoid on the floor. By the time Ilka and Donald arrived with the lights, she was rocking a miniature Person in her arms. A Baby.

Carmen had never seen one before, outside of Medical texts. She regarded it with awe, examining its tiny fingers and toes. "Isn't it the most precious thing you've ever seen?" Most Precious screwed up his face and let out a bellow that, no doubt, could be heard two levels up.

Greg laughed at the surprise on her face. "Oh, definitely!"

There were five other babies in all, and Carmen had the privilege of taking two of them up in her arms. They were so tiny and delicate, she almost didn't trust Greg to carry one up until he informed her that he had babysat kids smaller and younger than this one, and once even twins. "And no," he said when she looked up horrified, "I didn't actually sit on them. I took care of them."

As they drew close to the soft circle of natural light in the Upper Sector, they heard David making plans to contact authorities to rescue the other Undergrounds across the face of the earth.

The babies had to be handed up through the entrance they had carved with the laser. Greg and Carmen, the last to emerge from the Underground, each needed a hand up, as well. By the time the two re-emerged into the fresh air, each of the babies had been claimed most happily by their Factors. One baby was even smiling. At Carmen.

Greg noticed her glance and drew her away from the crowd. It was nearing sunset again and the sky was scarlet and orange. Carmen shivered once, thinking about the Grand Overseer. He would have been discovered by this time, slumped over his desk. Lifeless. The Perfect World the Humanoids had planned would never be realized now.

A man walking by on the street stopped to stare at the strange gathering of pale-skinned refugees from the deep. Before moving on, he dropped the drippy thing he had been holding. *Litter.*

Carmen smiled radiantly up into Greg's face. No, it was far from perfect and things would be hard for a while, but it was their world. All theirs....

The End

Glossary

Following are terms which appear in *Escape to the Overworld*. While anyone in the twenty-second century would understand them, explanations are given here out of courtesy to readers from the early Techno Age.

A-Stack: The cooling tower for any atomic reactor.

AlphaBeta 1.1: The twenty-second century computer language used by Programmers to develop the sequential instructions which direct all activity within a proscribed SysAdmin environment.

Ask: To offer a member of the opposite sex the opportunity to enter into the state of being the Chosen of the Asker.

Boogeyman: An imaginary evil hobgoblin supposed to carry off naughty children.

C-chime: A low-pitched, pleasant signal of thirty seconds duration which tells the Children of the Underground to go to their next area of duty; the Bell.

Californspeak: A bionic computer language developed in the late twentieth century by Silicon Valley technologists.

Chemohydrate: A Grade Thirteen subject covering chemical relationships which are based on H_2O.

Children, The: An age group of educable humans, between Babies and Factors, raised in the Underground by their Humanoid masters.

Chocobar: A small, self-contained snack, wrapped in paper or plastic, which is rich in the sweet, crystalline carbohydrate $C_{12}H_{22}O_{11}$ and the flavourful cacao seed pod, which dates back to the ancient Aztecs.

Chosen: A Child, of either sex, who has been Asked by a member of the opposite sex to enter into a relationship in a Factor Group for the purpose of childbearing; an engaged person.

Cobalt Wars: An internecine conflict in the early twenty-first century employing radioactive isotope warfare for the first time, resulting in generations of children with green and bluish-green eyes.

Creators: A small group of scientists of the late twentieth century who developed the Humanoids and mysteriously disappeared from the face of the earth shortly thereafter.

Day: The largest unit of time measurement (other than the variable *lifetime*) employed in the Underground; twenty-four hours.

Deact: To deactivate; to turn off.

Digitime: An omnipresent time readout on a computer screen or on an Underground wall which made personal timekeeping devices obsolete.

Drink: A liquid nutrient fed to the Children during Meals, employed to dissolve vitamins, essential trace elements, and other chemicals deemed necessary for the health of the Children by Humanoid nutritionists.

Durabuilt: A nuclear-proof building material of the twenty-second century.

Ear: A Humanoid device, usually small and difficult to detect, for monitoring organic vibrations and sounds.

Ellay: A city-state of Noram, located on the West Coast; the Central power for Humanoids.

Eye: Like the Ear, a Humanoid device for visually monitoring human-generated activity.

Factor Cubed: A factor of a factor of a factor; a great-grandparent.

Factor Group: A coset of Chosen Children, usually composed of five couples, which is the smallest number of Factors deemed efficient by the Humanoids for orderly reproduction of the human species.

Factor Squared: A factor of a factor; a grandparent.

Factor: A progenitor, of either sex, employed by the Humanoids to multiply the human race; a parent.

Food: A solid substance composed of proteins, minerals and other digestible nutrients deemed essential for the health of the Children by Humanoid nutritionists.

Grand Overseer: A supreme ruler of one of the city-states of the twenty-second century; a super-mayor.

Hologrammer: A three-dimensional digital display based on the principles of holography.

Humanoid: An artificially-intelligent robot resembling a human in shape, speech and action, developed by scientists in the late-twentieth century.

Keyterm: A computer console consisting of a video display terminal and a keyboard which has stand-alone and/or networking capabilities, depending on the application.

L-Vate: A transportation device used to raise, lower and move people within and between buildings.

Meal A: The Children's first nutritional intake of the Day; breakfast.

Meal B: The Children's second nutritional intake of the Day; lunch.

Meal C: The Children's last nutritional intake of the Day; supper or dinner.

Medi-data: A chart containing medical information on a patient.

Meganeutronic Saturation: Enormous destruction of life by Neutron Bombs.

Miliforce: The combined land, sea and air forces of a politically-described area; any super-army.

Motor-area Board: The computer component, located in the head, which directs robotic thoughts and motions; a Humanoid's brain.

Networking Protocols: Agreed-upon conventions which govern the transmission of infodata among a varying number of keyterms within the same computing environment.

Neutrino: An elementary particle in physics which has zero rest mass and charge, emitted in certain radioactive-decay processes; something really tiny and hard to find.

Neutron Bomb: A nuclear explosionary device of the twentieth century that releases a fatal neutron shower of low-level contamination allowing the target area to be occupied and used in a normal manner shortly after the detonation of the said device; an N-bomb.

Newcomer: A human, born of the Overworld and introduced into the Underground for purposes of childbearing.

Noram: The geopolitical area of continental North America.

Overworld: The surface of the Earth.

Programmer: A gigantic computer which not only processes keyterm infodata, but has a life of its own, governed only by SysAdmin rules.

Project: A workshop seminar in which the Children learn at the same time as they work in the Underground.

Psychocybernetics: The study of mental control functions and the application of statistical mechanics to human thought and action; mind-snatching.

Psychometry: A Humanoid method of measuring mental purity in humans.

Psychosoothe: To calm an agitated human by using musical sounds and encouraging words; to sing a lullaby.

Psychosurgery: The practice of treating a Removee's behaviour problems by using lasers on certain lobes of the brain to bring about selective amnesia.

Radioactivites: Vitamins which raise the human body's resistance to the effects of radioactivity.

Rebar: A bendable metal, around which cement is poured, that lends tensile strength to a concrete wall, floor or roof.

Remove: To withdraw a human from Underground society for the purpose of behaviour modification through the use of psychosurgery.

Removee: One who has been Removed.

Return: To introduce a Removee back into Underground society.

Sleeptime: The period of time in a Day devoted to both mental and physical downtime; going to bed.

SysAdmin: The system administration of a Programmer; that which controls the controller in a computer.

Teleportation: A form of public transport developed in the twenty-first century which reduces patrons to their component atoms at one station and microwaves them to the selected destination where they are reassembled.

Tri-Dynamics: A Underground Project devoted to the branch of mechanics which deals with the motion and equilibrium of systems under the three major exterior forces of time, space and gravity; a hard course.

Tronno: A twenty-first century city-state founded on the ruins of the ancient Eastern Canadian city of Toronto.

Underground, The: Secret bomb shelters far below the surface of the earth, constructed in the second half of the twentieth century, but now used to house the Children.

Urban Legend: Bizarre but believed tales told as truth, similar to the story of the Ellay housewife who, in a hurry to dry off her poodle which fell in the swimming pool, put him into the microwave; untrue stories.

Verdeocrystal: The active component in a lightweight laser, only producible under weightless conditions.

Videosim: An educational device which simulates real-life situations on a keyterm.

Warning: A verbal Punishment of a human, usually one of the Children, by a Humanoid who has detected a behavioural problem; if Disobeyed, leads to being Removed.

ABOUT THE AUTHOR

Nicole Luiken

Nicole Luiken was born May 25, 1971, in the small town of Manning, Alberta. She was raised on a farm in nearby Hawk Hills. The love of literature touched her first as a reader. Beginning with Nancy Drew, the Hardy Boys and Agatha Christie, Nicole now enjoys Alistair MacLean, Gordon Korman and Piers Anthony, but confesses she'll "read any book under the sun providing it's well written."